THE DAUGHTERS OF MEN

By

Richard Ankony

Preface

This sci-fi thriller and romantic love story is about the return of "the sons of God" for their harvest, "the daughters of men" at the end of this present age which is today.

It is an affirmation of the "ancient astronaut theory" of what transpired before the "Great Flood" and before the creation of men.

This book will explain the reasons for the frequent and increasing appearances of the Gigantopithecus, the Yeti and Sasquatch, who are the original indigenous beings of the planet Earth and why now they want to retake it back at all cost.

This novel will also address why there has been, why there is and why there will be such an insatiable, passionate, romantic and unbroken enduring desire between "the daughters of men" and "the sons of God."

As an Anunnaki Warrior Prince, from the planet Nibiru whose earth name is, Captain Frank Legion, U.S.M.C., I do hereby instruct my scribe, Rashid Anon, of the Supreme Council, a descendant from the Great Hall of my people to inform you of our presence and to relay events that will soon come to pass.

So let it be written.

So let it be done.

Dedication:

To my dear mother whose boundless love awaits me with open arms and eager anticipation, at the banquet, in the Great Hall of my people.

Rashid Anon

"And it came to pass, when men began to multiply on the face of the earth, and daughters were born unto them, that the sons of God saw the daughters of men that they were fair; and they took them wives of all which they chose.

There were giants in the earth in those days; and also after that, when the sons of God came in unto the daughters of men, and they bare children to them, the same became mighty men, which were of old, men of renown." Genesis 6:1

Chapter 1-In the Beginning

How could you have known?

For the world has changed since then and none now live of your race that remember it. For that which once was known on earth, in time gone by, has become lost and forgotten. For the history of my race, the Anunnaki, known in Genesis of your Holy Bible, as the *"sons of God"*, had become myth and myth has become legend.

Nevertheless, We, the Anunnaki, were here 450,000 years ago and 100,000 years before your creation.

Now this is the story of your past and what happened, so remember it well, for we go back now in time past when our ancestors created your race 350,000 years ago in a time and place since forgotten.

Why did we, *"the sons of God"* mate with *"the daughters of men?"*

It began this way, in the olden times; there were world wars on our home planet, Nibiru, the tenth planet in your solar system. The males of my Anunnaki's race became almost exterminated to the last male as tribe fought tribe for power and control of the planet.

Due to numerous nuclear wars on our planet, conditions became deteriorated to such a degree that the Supreme Council from the Great Hall of my people brokered and negotiated a peace treaty among the warring factions and tribes.

Because of the near extermination of the male species, the conditions were such on our planet that our race was approaching extinction, which demanded our utmost attention for the matter to be addressed and resolved.

The Supreme Council decreed that in order to preserve our dying race; a procreation process would have to be implemented to overcome the appalling death attrition rate through war. It was then decided, that female harems would be allowed under law and that male Anunnaki's could choose as many female counterparts as they could support.

This ancient ruling has been kept in place and has been handed down until today on your planet as demonstrated in the Middle East.

For our planet, Nibiru, development was much similar to your earth during the Great War of World War II, where millions of Russian and German men died on the battlefield in wars of attrition and extermination. This war along with World War I, the Great War to end all wars, in turn created millions of heartbroken and unmarried women on both sides of the battlefield to live out their lives in despair and loneliness.

Due to these constant wars on our planet the attrition rate of our males left them almost non-existent. So much so, that our females became dominant in the work force and further became the breadwinner of the family, for there was little to no males left.

At this time many of the females on our planet began to metamorphosize into something, which did not exist before, for they looked like females but acted like men. Because our females had nothing to naturally mate with they gave up on attempting to improve their natural beauty or stay sexually attractive. They first changed into something neuter, neither woman nor man without the soft feminine traits but rather they became a thing, or better said "a creature" which had no intrinsic value for our race.

The males that were left who had survived the wars of our race, for the most part, became smaller and puny in statue as if they were little boys with little to no masculinity.

The males developed a subculture where they desired each other for they were intimidated by having sex with the larger females.

As time passed these undeveloped males later became known as the "Sisters", for their desire to mate with females became almost non-existent.

Like the conditions that prevail on earth today, it was so on our planet also, for females had become overbearing and focused only on money, power and statue of their male counterparts.

This in turn caused the female's love for their male counterparts to become oppressive and cold for they had rejected even the few healthy males out of hand if they lacked power or money.

In their senselessness and irresponsibility the females desperately would mate with a lower order "beings" who dressed like males but were not males, in order to fulfill their sexual passions.

Once it was realized overall that these sexual trysts ended violently and the offspring of this "mixing" produced genetically regressive beings, the females en masse shortsightedly attempted to find love in the arms of other females in homosexual relationships.

These females then sought lesbian lovers, who understood them, for they carried a high degree of masculinity and filled the void of a loveless life.

These masculine females later became known as, "The Dykes" who were sexually used as a substitute male to satisfy the females twisted sexual demands and their misdirected passions.

The males in turn became fearful of the females, especially "The Dykes" so much so, that the breaking point came when the females would cannibalize their male counterparts.

The "Dykes" because of their animalistic and territorial nature hated the smaller males and began to murder the "Sisters" for any violation.

This continual backsliding continued to regress the genetics of our race and weakened it further almost beyond repair. This irresponsible and reckless conduct threw away millions of years of evolution that was painstakingly cultivated by my race. Our newborn children had shorter life spans and were born with diseases that were unknown to us at the time. After a period of time on our planet as our race finally started to procreate faster then our deaths, the females in our species became taller and stronger in statue then the weak males who had become biologically regressed by numerous wars.

These females resented the fact that they could not have their own males for themselves and they violently resented sharing their impotent males with other members of the female harem.

Females on our planet then became, cold, immoral, unethical, calculating, manipulative, loveless and predatory. The males did not desire these females and in secret conspired together for a means of escape.

Finally, in despair, the few remaining developed males fled their home planet, Nibiru, for safer sanctuaries elsewhere in the solar system without any intentions of ever returning. The males were brokenhearted for they had no mate and were terribly lonely.

The majority of males who escaped Nibiru committed suicide rather then live a meaningless life alone with a broken heart in the dark and frigid emptiness of space.

Many of our males who were found frozen to death on the tundra's on the "out planets" of our solar system died from deliberate starvation.

Death was refuge for them and the darkness and coldness of space embraced them with eternal sleep.

Our race again headed toward imminent extinction without a chance of recovery.

Our race, the Anunnaki race, had then reached its lowest point in its known history of millions of years and was teetering on the brink of becoming totally extinct.

On the home planet, Nibiru, the females would look for real males to mate with but there were none to be found anywhere.

The females wept bitterly and realized the error of their ways for they died childless and alone until the end of their days.

Because of this backsliding and constant warring without any consideration for peace, it was viewed as an abomination in the heavens where chastisement was decreed from the *"Eternal One of All."*

Natural disasters upon disasters fell upon our planet in the form of super volcanoes, earthquakes and the destruction of our atmosphere's stability, which was needed to maintain our climate and food harvest.

Our race was dying and therefore in order to bring climate stabilization to our planet we needed to obtain gold to protect our atmosphere. Through space exploration only your earth was found to contain gold in sufficient amounts to save our planet and race.

We needed to harvest gold from your planet but our workers were few, so we took the original ape-man, the Gigantopithecus, from your planet that was put there by God of the Universe and mixed our genes with them to create man, as an intelligent worker hybrid.

Your race, the human race, is a hybrid byproduct of the mixing of the Gigantopithecus and my race, the Anunnaki.

As our needs became more sophisticated we constantly upgraded your race by destroying the genetically regressive hominids among you, so that your race may advance according to our needs.

We have made you as a worker slave race, yet as time passed, you had become inseparable from us and genetically identical to us in many ways.

A symbiotic relationship developed between our races, that is, we both needed each other to survive and this is where we stand presently.

What had happened to us in ages past is now occurring to the human race today.

That is, evil is rampant throughout your world and war is always on the horizon and men have become women and women have become men.

Moreover, the human race is reverting back to its hominid stage in its habits and ways due to a lack of infusion of our Anunnaki genetics back into the human gene pool.

One of the best indicators of human regression is the animal characteristic for deviant sexual acts, which is in fact a genetic regression back to the hominid stage of the Gigantopithecus.

This in turn will compel the human race to revert back to its original form, the Gigantopithecus, as the Anunnaki gene pool becomes less and less prevalent in the human admixture.

This is the reason why there is such an increase in unusual sexual deviance among humans today for unbeknown to them they are reverting back to the hominid stage they originated from, which is the Gigantopithecus.

For did not Cain who murdered Abel in your holy book given a mark by the lord of the earth to protect him from the lower order hominids that existed outside of the gates of the Garden of Eden?

Even Cain knew then, those beings, the Gigantopithecus, were lower order hominids and intuitively refused to mate with them. This problem of mating with lower order "beings" is being conducted today primarily by some senseless women who are more concerned about raising their own social status instead of honoring the sacred ritual of marriage for love, child procreation and protecting their genetic heritage.

What good is a woman if she is the salt of the earth yet has lost her taste?

Moreover, what will become of her children who will now carry the genetic characteristics of a regressive being with all their uncured diseases?

Nevertheless, the only possible reversal of this situation is a massive injection of Anunnaki genes to reverse this regressive tide. However, this cannot happen now for the end of the age is upon you as has been prophesized in your holy book.

As the turbulence continued on our planet the Supreme Council in an attempt to return back to the sacred order of mating and marriage decreed that all male Anunnaki return to Nibiru at once, to mate and procreate or be subject to the death penalty.

The "out planets" males *refused* and decided to stand together against the decree and accepted death before abuse or enslavement by the feminists "Dykes."

The males hid throughout the "out planets" and built a society in the caves on Mars. Due to the males warlike nature in their past they had become experts in warfare and therefore built advance weapons for their defense against the "Dykes" who were ordered to round them up.

Using these advance techniques for warfare, the Anunnaki males, decided once and for all to annihilate all the females "Dykes" of their species…for they had enough!

So much so, that a blood oath was sworn among all the males that every "Dyke" female should be put to death without mercy if captured and not be allowed to return back to Nibiru.

The male Anunnaki's set up super sophisticated ambush and annihilation strategies which was to be implemented against any approaching Nibiru ships looking for them.

As anticipated the Nibiru ships came in force with "The Dykes" females in their jackboots as the advance guard to gather the males and enslave them.

But the males killed them, as they approached the "out planets."

"The Dykes," returned again and again as ordered to the "out planets" yet the remnant of Anunnaki males killed all of them, for none returned back to Nibiru.

The Great Council realizing that their decree had failed granted any Anunnaki males "off planet" a pardon so that they would not be condemned to death if they would just return to their home planet.

The Anunnaki males on the "out planets" still *refused* to return and stood unified together against any decree from Nibiru.

The Anunnaki males on the "out planets" sent transmissions stating that they were going to exterminate the whole planet of Nibiru including the females for their transgressions against them.

The Great Council from the Great Hall and the Anunnaki's from Nibiru were very concerned "for a house divided against itself cannot stand" and therefore realized conditions had gotten so far out of control that the lions were coming back to kill the lioness's pride without mercy.

The "out planet" Anunnaki males demanded that all feminists "Dykes" on Nibiru be put to death but the council from the Great Hall of our people…. refused.

The natural female Anunnaki's wept bitterly and became suicidal, finally realizing what had happened, these females took a sacred oath among themselves that all males returning to their planet would not be harmed by any female under penalty of death to that female.

Moreover, the female would once again honor their male counterparts as a loving spouse to be cherished and held in high esteem.

With this oath, some "out planet" males returned back to Nibiru to procreate; yet many of them still would not return for they feared a trap by "The Dykes."

It was at this point, that "the sons of God" looked down upon the earth and seen that "the daughters of men" were fair and beautiful, as stated in Genesis of your Holy Bible.

For "the daughters of men" were untainted and enjoyable to be with and they loved the "son's of God" with all their heart, which in turn brought great joy and comfort to the Anunnaki males.

It was then, that the "sons of God" took "the daughters of men" as wives, not because they were malicious abductors or evil but because they were lonely and needed companionship. They wanted romance as in the ancient times of days gone by and a warm-blooded female to hold and caress until the end of their days.

Yes, they did enjoy "the daughters of men" and they bore the Anunnaki males children, men of renown.

Yet the Anunnaki were not evil, as believed fallen angels, but rather just starving for love, romance and companionship.

For life without love, life was meaningless.

What were they, the Anunnaki males to do?

For even, the **Lord of Heaven** stated the greatest of all things **is love,** for is this not written in your holy book, the Bible?

It was at this time, that the Eternal **God** of Heaven dispatched an ambassador warning us to return back to our own females and leave *"the daughters of men"* to *"the sons of men."*

We refused!

We then were punished and condemned as **fallen angels** of which we were not. God's punishment was decreed upon us up to the time of deluge in the days of Noah, which occurred 13,500 years ago for mating with *"the daughters of men."*

We witnessed the deluge of Noah's day, when the earth's atmosphere changed drastically with a lower atmospheric pressure, then with lower oxygen levels and finally higher levels of solar radiation.

These three primary factors are why the human's life span has declined from approximately 1,000 years before the flood to 120 years after the flood.

To complicate matters even more, our offspring on earth, we found were contaminated with the genes of men, which was found to be unacceptable by the Supreme Council from the Great Hall of my people.

Those Anunnaki's found with less then 75% Anunnaki blood could not return to Nibiru.

We were then alone with our families rejected like lepers from our planet, for many of us had less then 75% Anunnaki genes!

Left to fend for ourselves because our offspring were part human we were then forced to live on Earth, the Moon and Mars.

Some of us with near 75% Anunnaki genetics went deep into the ocean to decrease our solar radiation and to increase pressure like on our home planet so as to attempt to maintain our long life span of nearly 500,000 earth years.

Those of us with 66% Anunnaki genetics as was Gilgamesh and Alexander the Great lived within the inner earth by accessing the earth's poles and resided with the Giganthepitechus who lived **in** the earth as it is written.

Lastly, there were those of us who had 50% or less of Anunnaki genetics who were grievously affected by the sun's solar radiation, decreased atmospheric pressure and lower oxygen levels that our life span was drastically reduced to a mere few hundred years.

We then had to live near the area of the Anunnaki space-landing place Baalbek, Lebanon (Sun City) and reside there in the village of Ankoun near Masgara not far from Beirut.

Our last name in part is **Anon**, Aon, Anune, Anoune or Anun a direct offspring of our ancestors the Anunnaki from which Abraham and *Keturah, his wife* originated.

We therefore are an ancient people who have walked among you on earth for nearly 350,000 years.

We too were rejected like lepers until the end of this age, which is upon us now where *The Lord of Heaven,* promise to redeem us.

For the cataclysm must come as it had in the days of Noah. For is it not written in your holy book, "Behold I maketh the earth desolate, I maketh it empty, I turneth the earth upside down and scattereth the inhabitants therein?"

Was not Baalbek, a Cedar garden of Lebanon, a landing place for Anunnaki ships and paradise, your Garden of Eden?

For is this not also written in your holy book about the King of Tyre from a city-state on the coast of Lebanon.

Surely you have read that the Lord God stated to the King of Tyre in Ezekiel 28:13, "That you were in Eden, the garden of God…. you were on the holy mountain of God."

Surely you read this in the bible about paradise and Baalbek.

I, Rashid Anon, an offspring of our ancestors the Anunnaki, the children of Masgara and Ankoun, Lebanon, tell you this.

We are the offspring of our ancestors, the Anunnaki, and the union of Abraham and Keturah.

Now, you people of the earth know who *the sons of God* are and what happened to them and their offspring.

Prepare yourselves for the time is at hand.

I, Rashid Anon, an appointed scribe in the Supreme Council from the Great Hall of my people, the Anunnaki, have now completed my directed mission and divine task to inform the people of the earth as instructed by our anointed warrior prince so named below.

Frank Legion-Anon
An Anointed Anunnaki Warrior Prince

<u>Chapter 2-The Return</u>

Funny how life is, like the saying goes, *up in fame, down in flames,* has led me to wonder what would the next year bring?

In one moment of time I'm standing in high cotton like a conquering Roman hero while in the next moment, I'm lying somewhere in the shadows of black bottom.

Some things are hard to explain but mistakes happen.

Some people blame it on my lady friend, Nikki, while others say; I was showboating to get my name in the lights of Broadway.

But, how was I to know?

Things go wrong, you can't control it, you can't predict it…. it just happens and you are left to live with the consequences.

It was the seventh game of the World Series, the Detroit Tigers vs. the San Francisco Giants.

The Giants were leading 4-0, with the Tigers at bat with one out and bases loaded in the bottom of the ninth.

The whole season was at stake as I walked from the on deck batting circle to the plate.

The roar of nearly 50,000 screaming fans sounded as if the thunder gods themselves were yelling out my nickname, *"Legatus, Legatus,"* as I stepped up to the plate, in my Detroit Tigers uniform.

I was overwhelmed by the fanaticism of the crowd for even the ground shook beneath my feet from their roar as I walked towards the plate.

As I stood at the plate staring down this farm boy, a southpaw from Nebraska, I couldn't help but wonder how this showdown was going to end.

So, I took the first two smoking fastballs right down the middle as the ump screamed out, STRIKE!

The big southpaw confident he was going to drop me on strikes scanned the runners and nodded in the affirmative the sign from the catcher as he started his wind-up to seal my fate. In a flash the southpaw sent another smoker right down the middle of which I engaged squarely with every ounce of my strength and hit the ball to straight away center field for a bases loaded three run triple, putting the Tigers within reach of tying the score, 4 to 3.

As I stood at third base enjoying a standing ovation from the thunderous crowd, I waved my hat to them in appreciation.

As like everything in the fog of war, my mind became focused on the jubilant crowd instead of the game.

It was then that I picked up the signal from the dugout to steal home plate on the next pitch while I looked back at the third base coach bewildered while looking for verification.

I said to myself, "What the…"

The third base coach nodded in the affirmative.

"Hell, here goes," I said to myself, "All or nothing."

The Giants, southpaw pitcher again true to form fires another smoking fastball, which our powerhouse player, Ben Gulp, pops it up into the catchers mitt, making two outs, as I make my break for home plate like a runaway freight train barreling down for the tying run, when suddenly I realized that I got my signals crossed and I was to run only on a successful bunt.

As they say the rest is history, as this Giant's catcher looks at me, a fool, running down the base path at him with no chance to make the plate without being tagged out.

And out I was!

The 50,000 screaming fans became dead silent and you could hear a pin drop. The home plate umpire screamed out, "*Your out of here Legion!*"

I can't express the feeling I felt as the Giants players began jumping up and down in front of me celebrating winning the World Series. As I'm laying face down in the dirt, looking at home plate two feet from my nose, all worldwide television cameras broadcasting the World Series were upon me.

I can't explain how bad I felt, I'm stunned and silent as 50,000 Detroit fans stared at me in utter shock as I lay there.

The crowd was so numb that they couldn't boo me and I couldn't lift myself up to look them or the world in the face.

I just sat there in my shame, as the Giants ballplayers dancing all around me laughing and celebrating forgot I was even there.

Finally, Ben Gulp walked up to me and lifted me up out of the dust and walked me back to the dugout with his arm over my shoulder.

As the saying goes, a person really doesn't know life until one experiences it from both sides of the fence for victory has a thousand fathers but defeat is an orphan.

Damn, this side is ugly, bone dead coyote ugly, how could the fans and I ever forget it.

Now I, Captain Frank "*Legatus*" Legion, U.S.M.C., sat incognito feeding the pigeons from a bench in Central Park, Manhattan, returning to reality after reflecting about that critical game.

I wondered if my baseball career as a left fielder with the Detroit Tigers had abruptly ended. Especially with my call up from the military reserves to respond immediately to advanced military pilot training at Naval Air Station Meridian, Mississippi which may prevent me from returning back to baseball, my boyhood dream.

With classified secrecy I was dispatched to a fighter squadron where I completed my first tour of duty. While I was dispatched to this classified assignment in the East China Sea arena in the Far East, I flew combat missions with a highly secretive Navy/Marine combat fighter squadron.

As fate would have it after my last dismal performance with the Detroit Tigers, I was immediately sent into combat where the thunder gods of heaven returned to shine down on me once again.

My successful combat performance had affected my very private lifestyle, which suddenly was cast into the glamour and stardom of Hollywood. I was classified, as "Celebrity 1A status" which I was told was as high as you could get in "Tinsel Town."

If that was not enough the bright lights of Broadway would not take second fiddle and I was invited on all major prime time shows.

I didn't like this new life but the nation and free world needed some heroes and I was along with some of my friends chosen to fill this void for our heroism in combat in the Far East campaign, known only as the "People's War."

For the "Peoples War" had taken my life to new and uncharted areas where I reached "Ace" status, as a fighter pilot, by downing sixteen enemy combatants believed by the public to have occurred somewhere over the uninhabited Senkaku Islands in the East China Sea.

In the process, myself and my so called "human buddies", Lt. Joe "Hitman" Calloway, U.S.N. and Lt. Billy "Boot" Hill, U.S.N. each won the Congressional Medal of Honor for defending, the nuclear aircraft carrier, USS Ronald Regan from being destroyed by enemy combatants who were carrying anti-ship missiles.

"Boot" looked like the actor Bill Paxton and "Hitman" reminded me of the actor William Defoe from the movie, Platoon, as for me I was just tall dark and handsome.

The combatants in the press were assumed to be Russian and Chinese Mig fighters…but those in the know, knew better.

Yet, the saving of so many American lives, by "Boot", "Hitman", and myself, was so appreciated by the American people that we three officers were given a full-blown ticker tape parade, which was only rivaled by the return of General MacArthur.

As I sat there on my park bench in my solitude I wondered about my invitation today on the Bettermen Show, for I did not want to make a fool of myself again as in the World Series. While sitting there reminiscing in a trance like state as I stared at the pigeons I was moved by the fragrance in the air of cedar wood burning which reminded me of the campfires at the front.

The music of "Bobby Darins, Beyond the Sea," filled the air, causing my mind to further drift to "happy thoughts" and reminisce of Capt. Nikki Aliz, U.S.M.C., when I first saw her.

Her, 5'8" inch frame, with those smoldering brown eyes and radiant dark brown hair blowing in the wind was like a gentle warm breeze swaying a palm tree. Her graceful walk flowed in synchronous coordination and those long silky tanned legs of hers captivated me. She was a mature and gorgeous brunette that was highly educated who was in the process of becoming a Catholic nun, but left the nunnery and marriage proposals to take care of her sickly mother. Her kindness and her soft tender kisses were always unforgettable…. I do miss her so.

For indeed, there are something's that only a woman could fill in a man's heart. Damn, I hate being alone all the time with my dreams.

As I returned back to my reality, I wondered about the wisdom of the Supreme Council regarding my two fold mission at hand of defending this planet from alien hosts and to find a woman in question that they wanted for procreation purposes.

According to Nikki who was assigned to Naval Intelligence, informed me that a gigantic alien race of immeasurable size from outside our galaxy was spotted in the rings of Saturn and in the southern quadrant of our moon. Their status and intent was unknown but believed by our intelligent agencies to be hostile and incoming.

To make matters worse the ancient inhabitants and indigenous hominids of the earth, the *Gigantopithecus,* had made it clear through diplomatic channels that the earth was theirs and they wanted it back.

During the period of the flood of "Noah," the *Lord of Heaven* had 85,000 of the indigenous Gigantopithecus killed off for raping "the daughters of men" by splitting them open during sexual intercourse and for eating humans alive.

Since their eviction from the earth, the Gigantopithecus waited out their allotted time as set by the *Lord of Heaven* before returning to the earth to retake their planet and to enslave the human race.

The Gigantopithecus were first detected in the caves on Mars about the same time the gigantic beings known as "The Giants" were spotted within the rings of Saturn.

"The Giants" in their incomprehensible enormous size ships had left our top scientists to speculate that the present human homo-sapien-sapien and my species, the Anunnaki, had been deliberately micro-shrunk sometime in the past.

"The Giants" had reached the southern dark side of earth's moon in scout ships that were ten times the size of Los Angeles. No one knew if this was a coordinated attack or a prelude to extraterrestrial races testing our resolve to resist a full-scale invasion?

We hoped that "The Giants" were advanced robots on a mining expedition on the moon but we didn't know, so we built up our defenses and challenged their offensive probes.

Despite all these thoughts going through my head, I couldn't help but enjoy the warmth of the sun, the smell of tasty food and the sight and fragrance of long legged women who were dressed to the nines in their silky short dresses as they walked by me as if I were invisible.

Earth women, they have become so elegant, fashionable and well-bred now, what man could resist their splendor and charm…. simply irresistible.

They were so beautiful, eloquent and sophisticated that their very presence excited me. No wonder, my forefathers the "sons of God" loved them so, yet despite all their beauty they made themselves so unreachable now and were becoming more and more like the females on my home planet, Nibiru.

Like my ancestors, the Anunnaki, known as the "sons of God" were before me, I totally understood how they felt about these fair earthly beauties "the daughters of men" which my grandfathers chose as wives as many as they desired. Indeed the women were fair and tantalizing especially those advanced hybrids with sandy blonde hair.

Yes, as a matter-of-fact a fair and sandy blonde came out of Africa from the nation today called South Africa. Fair means not dark and that's exactly what it meant *"for the sons of God saw the daughters of men that they were fair; and they took them wives of all which they chose."*

What is not known is that the Gigantopithecus, also known as Sasquatch, and Bigfoot, had blond hair, and when crossbred with the dark haired Anunnaki, the blond hair carried over to the human hybrids.

Now as then, the time of mating in my culture was a male's ritual and my time had come to select an earthly female that delighted me and also had the predominant genetic characteristics of my race to satisfy the high counsel.

For it was critical for my species to enrich itself by introducing a more diverse genetic gene pool between my race and "the daughters of men."

In essence, I was on a mission looking for a highly evolved woman and from her; we would become molds for a new race of hybrid beings.

As I sat there admiring these fair beauties, I became overwhelmed by their natural fragrance, that is their scent, for which my senses were more highly evolved and able to detect at a far greater range then earthly men.

Their cologne and scent aroused my appetite and hunger, which only a female could create and fulfill.

No wonder my ancestors feasted on these beauties…they were then and still are…. wonderful to behold.

The harvest had come and not a second to soon for the earth was becoming more violent and wicked by the moment and our species as in the past had to select the best of the selected seeds of "the daughters of men" for further procreation.

For as it was in the days of Noah so it is now at the end of the age, a great cataclysm was coming, yet the people of earth were asleep and drunk with corruption for they could no longer see the signs of the time but only the signs of the weather.

As in time gone by at the last deluge only a few selected seeds were chosen from the multiple diverse people who then roamed the earth.

Now as back then it was my sacred duty to find my selection, my elect, for she was to be my mate forever. For other males from my race were now here on Terra Firma on the same covert mission as me for our time was short and disappointment and risks were high.

For we must select during this time frame our designated daughter of man who is a hybrid descendant from my ancestors and the God made ape, the hominid, Gigantopithecus.

These genetically desired women chosen by the Supreme Council from the Great Hall of my people have found certain earthly women to have evolved genetically and become sophisticated enough to procreate to a higher evolved species.

Knowing that time was short for the people of the earth, I had no time to lose and as the mating ritual demanded, a sacred oath from time everlasting had to be honored. Our sacred oath demanded that our selected female must choose us freely and not be taken against her will. Furthermore, our selected mate besides choosing us freely must believe she has chosen us as her mate for life.

I couldn't help to ponder and wonder how this beauty would look like and act, and if her senses were evolved enough to detect my pheromones which were many times more persuasive then men of the earth.

For we, Anunnaki could selectively intensify our pheromones and further selectively direct it to any desired female of our choosing.

For earth women have become much more sophisticated since the days of Noah for they have evolved more spiritually and sexually with more developed senses.

They could now detect our pheromones at greater distances if they carried our advance genetic female genes from my race.

As I looked away from watching the pigeons that were running between my feet, I wondered if my selected one would be morally and ethnically correct as was mandatory by the high council.

For any female with a feminist mentality or one with characteristic traits of "The Dykes" was rejected out of hand.

As I stared at the pigeons my two imperial guards from the Great Hall of my people, Omega and Tron, approached me in their black trench coats. Both of these guards were near seven feet tall and assigned as my protectors who were handed down to me by the ancient ones of old which created my race.

"Captain, she approaches." Omega stated.

"Where?" I stated as I scanned the multitude of women walking.

"South-South West, 200 meters and closing, Captain." Omega stated.

"She approaches with an entourage of armed guards and press people." Tron stated.

"Captain, the guards are heavily armed, should we stay with you?" Omega asked.

"No, you must not, for I must test her senses for genetic compatibility, without her being aware of my presence. So go now to your selected location within range of me and keep me apprised of any changing variables." I stated.

Omega stated, "Her name is Kate Winely. The council has informed us, Captain, that Kate is both morally and ethically correct and has not desecrated her body with graffiti nor mated with lower order humans.

Moreover, she is a God fearing woman with southern Baptist habits and characteristics. She appears to be highly suitable for your mission."

Tron replied, "We go now captain?"

I crossed my right arm across my heart and nodded my approval for them to leave for their designated location.

Suddenly, as I searched through the crowd, I could see her through the sun swept trees as she approached. She was tall and beautiful with long blonde hair and slender silky legs. As she walked with her entourage towards me discussing business of the day, I could see she was a movie star and a model as my guards had already informed me.

I began to pick up her essence, which aroused my pheromones and propelled me into ecstasy.

Looking away from her now, so in order to not attract her attention, I kept looking down at the pigeons that I was feeding.

As she walked by, I raised my eyes to observe her as she passed by me.

As she walked by me, her beauty was radiant, her smiling green eyes, which was, elongated as that of a cat, captivated me. Her voice was that of an innocent girl waiting to be transformed into a woman since time eternal that needed to be awakened from her slumber.

Her facial figures were well sculptured which revealed to me that she had strong ancient characteristics from my female ancestors. Her inner being, I could detect was more beautiful then her outer beauty, a perfect mate I thought, as I became overwhelmed with her scent.

I became hungry, very hungry.

As she continued to walk by me, my pheromones became violently activated and began charging to capacity. My focus was on her and her alone, for I must transmit my pheromones unilaterally at maxim intensity to determine the percentage of female Anunnaki genes that she was carrying from my ancestor's genetics.

The greater the distance that she could receive my pheromones, the greater degree of my race's characteristics she is carrying.

So I transmitted my pheromones at maximum distance and waited.

As she continued walking and discussing her business of the day, I could see no response from her and thought perhaps this beauty did not, after all, carry the advanced genetics of her creators.

Then suddenly, as she approached a cheering crowd to sign autographs, she stopped, and slowly turned herself around, as if someone she knew intuitively had called her name from a distance.

She had detected my presence and I could see she had become aroused, for she could sense me in the air and feel me through the earth.

Quickly I said to myself, I must not look at her, so I looked away from her direction so as not to reveal my identity.

Suddenly, the thought hit me and I became terrified, for this was impossible for her to detect my pheromones at this extreme range and is undocumented among "the daughters of men."

Something's wrong, but what?

"How could this be?" I said to myself, "For only a..........."

Then I became gripped with shear terror and terrified beyond all measure, "Oh my God," I thought, "She's a colony queen with almost 100% Anunnaki blood in addition to the blood of the ancient ones who created my race."

These extremely rare females are known as "Eve" for only a colony queen can detect at such distances.

She is a species and colony creator and at close range in a romantic episode her pheromones could fuse me to her in an act of passion and after mating kill me instantly if she so desires.

Why wasn't I told?

Why didn't the Supreme Council tell me of this?

Why?

She looked through the dense crowd in my direction, but her senses were not yet refined enough for the moment. She then returned to the cheering crowd who were screaming for her signatures and the paparazzi that swarmed around her for fashionable photographs.

In horror, I slipped away undetected calling my ancient guards Tron and Omega for an explanation.

<u>Chapter 3-And so it Begins</u>

As Tron and Omega approached me I could see they were as much shocked and concerned as I was. That is, how did this matter of a queen be given unto me without the council warning me of her dangers and significance?

"Tron and Omega," I angrily asked, "What is the meaning of this and why was your intelligence faulty?"

Omega replied, "Captain, we were unaware of this and nowhere in our intelligence briefing was it mentioned that you were pursuing a queen. We were blindsided just like you, Captain, on why would the council not make us aware of this important matter or brief us on the dangers of this detail."

Tron then interjected humbly, "We are sorry, Captain, we honestly did not know and are just as much concerned and shocked as you are. We have already forwarded a priority one dispatch for clarification on this matter to the Mars Way Station. We believe we will receive a suitable explanation on this critical matter very soon."

"Look," I stated, "You two are my Praetorian guards, the best of the best that has been given unto me to protect me from unseen dangers which is beyond my control. Therefore, if you cannot meet your mission objectives by informing me of grave dangers beyond my sensors, then what is your purpose?"

Both Tron and Omega looked hurt and gazed down at the ground.

Omega then stated, "We apologize Captain, it won't happen again, we promise this."

I then looked at Tron and Omega, realizing I was a bit harsh, "I'm sorry, Tron and Omega, you two are the best in the business and were personally given to me by the great council, forgive me?"

Omega stated, "Your apology is noted and accepted Captain."

Tron nodded in the approval.

Omega then stated, "Captain, you must now return to the apartment and change into your proper attire for the Bettermen Show. You have less then two hours to get ready for this appointment.

Be aware Captain when you return here you will be entering through the same studio door as that queen did.

Be advised Captain that the queen may be in the same studio and/or show with you."

"I thought about that already, Omega." As I scanned the sky, "So I could be at point-blank range if her sensors are on and she detects me. She could fuse me to her in front of a live audience, all the while blowing our presence and cover.

Sheesh, why can't I just get a normal woman to bed? I mean look at all these dolls walking around here dressed to the nines. I could have a feast with them, just like my ancestors did.

But, no, I get the black widow that can devour me which is deja vu of the women on our planet, in days gone by."

Tron and Omega chuckled, yet understood the severity as I walked back to my safe house to prepare myself for the show.

Once my cover is in the open I would be drawing large crowds of veterans and patriots in general, especially the second amendment, right to bear arms people. For as a veteran they believed I am one of them and therefore supportive of their political views. They could express themselves through me, a national hero, to promote their agenda of which I couldn't really blame them.

When I finished changing, I walked down to Studio 57 for my appearance that was within a half-hour. I was pre-briefed that the focus of my conversation would be about the battle in the East China Sea Theater.

I was further instructed by U.S. Naval Intelligence and my people from the Anunnaki Mars Way Station Intelligence Group to not veer from the subject matter so as not to alarm the people of the earth to the truth.

As I entered into the studio, after signing autographs and having my picture taken with political figures and veterans I was invited in and escorted to a staging area to await my turn to go on stage.

As I sat there waiting my turn in which I was told was second behind Kate Winely, the queen, I couldn't help but feel sick at heart that she could microwave me in front of a national audience.

I was waiting to hear her introduction so I could be informed of her story line and get the feel and the mood of the crowd. Omega approached me and whispered in my ear that there might be, due to the "People's War", anti-war demonstrators in the crowd.

"So be it," I said.

Suddenly, as I sat there, a black stage manager walked by me escorting this raving blonde beauty to the staging area to enter on stage. As I watched her walk by me in her knee high jump suit and gentle sway, damn was she breathtaking.

I said to myself if only I could land this doll. What a sweetheart and feast this would be to wake up to for the rest of her days.

I was becoming sexually aroused as I admired her long slender legs and graceful form.

I could feel my pheromones starting to recharge to such a point that at this range she may be able to detect me, so I tried to change my focus by looking at the colored stage lights above the curtains.

As I sat there trying to gaze upward, Kate without explanation turned and stared at me, my god, she was beautiful.... I couldn't turn away as I looked at her.

How does one express beauty in words? Her long blonde hair, dazzling smile with slender milky white legs in black high heels, overwhelmed me.

My God, I wish I could make love to that doll; no wonder women were called dishes...she really was delicious looking.

Her radiant beauty stunned me.

Oh my, I said to myself, "Why did God make them so divine like goddesses. This very thought started me to go into an uncontrollable pheromones fibulation. I was dead meat now if her sensors picked up my scent."

As I looked at her from the corner of my eye, I could see she was inquiring about me by asking the black stage manger who I was and why was I drawing larger crowds then her?

When he told her, she began looking at me with interest. I most definitely got her attention now and she was aware of my presence.

I then heard her say, "Is he the one?"

The black stage manger turned and looked at me stating, "That's what they say, Kate, he's the one."

Kate's appearance changed, from one of curiosity to a warm friendly smile.

I smiled back, then choked and shyly dropped my view to the floor, I was spellbound, a captive being, in her honey trap…. no way out but to surrender to her natural lure.

Oh my, I thought, what a fox, if I could just get a few moments with her and win her heart so as to make her mine forever.

Then I realized, that I must hide my desire from her…I must.

No wonder my ancestors were cast under a spell by the charm of *"the daughters of men."*

Suddenly, the stage announcement came for Kate as she turned her smiling eyes from me and commenced to walk on stage with her long legged model strut.

"My, what a beauty," I said, but I had to stay focused on my mission without upsetting it prematurely.

As I watched her enter on stage, it was readily apparent that the crowd loved her and adored her pure and girlish ways. Bettermen kissed her hand and gave her the first seat out of the three, which was closest to him.

Bettermen complimented her on her entrance and appearance.

I started to laugh as I watched Bettermen drool over her beauty.

They then discussed her movies, modeling and family life, which surely got the audiences attention.

At this time, I wondered if I was underdressed for this occasion by wearing just my military flight jacket over a white tee shirt, blue Wrangler pants and brown mountain shoes.

Too late to worry now when the drums are beating and the show passed to an advertisement intermission signaling my stage appearance was moments away.

The black manager then came up to me smiling and stated politely, "Mr. Frank Legion, your up to bat, are you ready?"

"Yes," I replied as I stood there at the on deck circle, feeling like a racehorse at the gates just before the gun is fired.

"Good," he replied, "Here we go."

As the advertisement ended, Mr. Bettermen mentioned my name to the crowd and asked them to give me a welcoming hand.

The crowd gave me a standing ovation at my appearance, which caught me totally off-guard.

For little did I know, that there were family members in the audience who had sons and daughters aboard the aircraft carrier USS Ronald Regan, where my two navy buddies and myself destroyed enemy hostiles who were attempting to attack the carrier.

The roar was deafening, to say the least, yet heart warming, as I thanked the crowd and turned to Mr. Bettermen to thank him for having me on his show.

I then gently shook Kate's hand and looked into her beautiful smiling eyes as she smiled back at me and moved to the second seat which would put my back to her as I talked to Mr. Bettermen.

As the crowd settled down and sat down, I asked Kate to please sit in the first seat and told her that I could never turn my back on a lady like her. Kate looked surprise and for a moment looked confused but respected my gentlemen's offer, thanked me and accepted it.

As she got up, almost embarrassed and crossed over to the first seat, her face came almost nose-to-nose with mine and in a microsecond a ping of information was transmitted between her riveting smiling eyes and mine.

I looked at her voluptuous lips and I became hungry…. I could taste her. Her natural female scent from a distance aroused my passions and created an instantaneous combustion within my soul.

I was on fire!

I wanted to seduce her right there and to hell with the consequences. I would plead insanity as an innocent victim overwhelmed from the scent of her nectar.

The men jurors would surely understand, as I laughed silently.

Oh my, I said, I can feel her sensors probing me, though she didn't know it.

Moreover, I could tell she was hungry and was awakening.

Then my mind switched back to reality and reminded me that I was on a mission for I did not come for a lovely face but rather for the grand eloquent woman on the inside who was carrying advance genes of my race with a natural strong desire to breed.

Mr. Bettermen immediately sensed the charisma between us but said nothing as we commenced with the show.

The crowd looked at us with curiosity but figured it was just a passing thing.

Mr. Bettermen then began asking me questions regarding "The Peoples War" and if I would return to baseball.

I dodged the baseball issue because I was still embarrassed but did discuss "The People's War" in favorable terms as Nikki from Naval Intelligence had directed me too.

Despite Mr. Bettermen's probing questions, I stayed focused on my mission for my tactical gambit had been put in motion, which was slowly being revealed. For every time I addressed Mr. Bettermen's questions, I would focus on Kate's smiling eyes at point-blank-range. So much so, that when the commercial intermission occurred Mr. Bettermen talked to the bandleader while Kate curiously slid over in her chair towards me as I continued to look at her as she stated, "Frank, what are you looking at?" as she gently smiled at me with all her female charm.

Whereby I looked into her laughing green eyes and I replied, "Why, I'm looking at you, Kate, I'm looking at you."

Kate's facial expression changed in a New York second, she intuitively moved her head away from me, like a King Cobra snake coiling. Yet with her beautiful radiant glow about her she looked intensely in my eyes as if searching for my soul as she reassessed her situation. At that very moment in time, the woman inside her was emerging and had become critically aware of my presence… and my hunger.

I was hunting her like a hunter, yet there was no indication that she was running. Why?

Kate's heart pounded as she moved her head back slightly away from me yet still fixated on my eyes. For a moment it looked as if Kate had seen a ghost as she took a deep breath.

The audience and Mr. Bettermen sensed the change of Kate's facial expression and wondered what was transpiring in front of them.

As the lighthearted conversation continued between us three, I leaned across Kate's chair and placed two tickets on Bettermen's desk. As I retracted myself and looked into Kate's eyes while our noses nearly touched, it took nearly every ounce of my power to control my pheromones and avoid being magnetically drawn into her irresistible lips.

I said to myself, "The hell with the crime, I'll do the time and it would be worth it…. shame on what *"the daughters of men"* do to their male counterparts, totally helpless we are, as I thought of the song "Simply Irresistible" by Robert Palmer."

Mr. Bettermen then asked me, "Oh…Frank what are these tickets for?"

I stated, "That's for you and your wife, Mr. Bettermen, or for Kate and her husband, boyfriend an opportunity to attend the Chief of Staffs Ball at the Kennedy Center Ballroom.

However, if neither of you can attend then perhaps have a raffle and give it to the crowd. There will be a lot of high-ranking officials there along with movie producers and noted celebrities."

Kate looked at me as I could sense the question she wanted to ask but hesitated.

"Interesting, and thank you by the way, Frank," Mr. Bettermen said, who then asked the question, "Why wouldn't you want to go, Frank, especially with your "Class 1A" celebrity status?"

I replied, "Well, I'm not much for the glamour of Hollywood, Broadway, or high society, Mr. Bettermen.

Plus, I just got in town with the 333rd Fighter Interceptor Squadron that just returned from deployment overseas and I don't know my way around town nor do I have a steady girl. So I'd rather not go alone."

Immediately an attractive woman in the audience yelled out, "I'll go with you!"

Everyone started laughing…. I just smiled, but said nothing.

Kate looked at me in a serious manner, which practically put me in a hypnotic trance…I had to have her…but how?

I was out of aces.

Suddenly, you could hear a pin drop as Kate looked at me then slowly turned her head towards Mr. Bettermen.

Placing her graceful hand on the desk stating, "I'll take them, Mr. Bettermen," she stated.

Kate turned her gaze towards me again and said, "I'll go with you?"

The females in the crowd were smiling now for they approved and wondered if this was the beginning of a romantic love affair.

It was!

Mr. Bettermen, also smiling, looking at me like I just hit pay dirt, slouched back in his chair, nodding in the affirmative as he relinquished the tickets to Kate.

I can't explain how I felt then, but I laughed silently within, when I thought about what "Boot" Hill told me once how his "chubby" would chew through his pants zipper and a chain link fence just to see a woman of his passion.

Indeed he was right for I felt my "chubby" had just jumped off its engine mount...damn; I needed a smoke and some fresh air. I was losing it and the fire down below was raging, man, what I'd do for a drag and a breather.

How can a woman move me this way?

Something must be wrong with me?

The God of heaven made them so appetizing, I had to shake my head, murmuring... it's not fair.

Back to reality, I stated, "You will?"

Kate softly stated, "Yes.... sure."

I stated, "That's wonderful Kate and though I've been at sea for six months, I promise I'll be a gentleman...I promise, I'll keep my hands to myself."

As I thought to myself, bullshit, I'll take the electric chair for a taste of your honey, baby, and I would be smiling when they dropped the 440 volts on me, saying, "Man their really cooking me now."

Kate just smiled and informed me she'll pick me up in her limo.

While everyone was looking around wondering if this was a predetermined deliberate trap I set for Kate or was it just my good fortune by getting "the rub of the green."

I did…for it was my destiny.

As our TV segment ended, Mr. Bettermen then introduced his third and last guest, which was some freak punk rocker that entered on stage. I could see he was a devolved bottom feeder from some heavy metal rock band who looked like he worked in the circus shoveling buffalo chips, with all of his tattoos.

Damn, but did the audience love him and gave this guy a standing ovation much better then Kate's and mine combined.

As the punk rocker approached Mr. Bettermen playing his guitar, the audience started dancing in the aisles. It was pandemonium to say the least.

Kate, out of politeness moved to the third seat from her first seat position, which was no place for a queen. While everyone in the audience, including Mr. Bettermen had their eyes on the kid rocker, as the audience began dancing with him, I had my eyes on Kate.

Kate began clapping her hands with stiff palms and split fingers like seal flippers for this musician. Yet despite her smile no one but her publicist and sub-publicist were paying her any mind. Yet, I could not take my eyes off her when she looked at me with her charming smile, a smile that you could believe in which pushed my blood to boiling.

Kate was here on a mission also which was to promote her upcoming movie in which she had a leading role, while a second blockbuster movie of hers was coming out within a few months, which the critics predicted might cast her into stardom.

With Kate to my back, I realized that this was my moment of a lifetime, my fate hung in the balance…. my eternity.

If not now…when?

If I fail here in this moment in time then I may dream alone for the rest of my life with broken dreams.

It was now or never.

Against this backdrop, I forgot the freak punk rocker and turned and talked to Kate instead, pursuing my destiny. As I looked at her during this enchanted evening across this crowded room, I knew both our fates would be determined in this split second of time…win or lose.

I got her attention by telling her how heavenly she looked and how her inner being was more beautiful and radiant then her exterior. In this small window of time I brought her to the center stage out of the corner she had been placed in.

I not only got the attention of her eyes but her soul also. It was in that specific point in time that our souls could exchange megabytes of data…. soul-to-soul.

Kate could see me now, as if blinders had been taken off her eyes…the woman has come forth…and she was hungry and wanted her man.

In that moment, I saw the innocence of a young girl, as virgin snow, which had been waiting since her creation by saving herself at a great expense for a man who was yet to come and awaken her from her eternal slumber.

For Kate's soul knew…. he must come…he must, for it is her destiny also.

And he was here…now!

In front of her, nose to nose!

As I gazed at Kate, I could see the colony queen strain in her, by the manner in which she carried herself. She had the virtue of a queen with dominant genes. She nodded and smiled at me, though not blushing, yet gracefully she thanked me politely for my compliments.

Kate further thanked me for not avoiding her in the third seat as a non-existent entity by paying attention to her despite the audience and Mr. Bettermen's focus elsewhere.

I then pulled a card out, as a backup plan, from my coat and told her in case she cancels out on the Chief of Staff ballroom dance with me, if she is ever in Nebraska near the Missouri border, I fly crop dusting planes in my spare time from Rick's Crop Dusting Service out of Farington Field, Nebraska.

I told her it's like being in heaven when flying over the corn and wheat fields in a biplane especially during the first light of sunrise.

"Kate," I told her, "If you ever get the chance for a little getaway bring your nephews, or whoever, and I'll give them a free ride in the backseat of a crop duster.

I promise your nephews or nieces would surely enjoy the ride if you can find the time. I'll even throw in a hot dog and a pop for all of you, if you come."

Her smiling eyes were radiant…. yet her demeanor was polite and professional and her intentions were yet unclear.

I left her the card on her armrest, hoping she would pick it up, I felt intuitively, though unsure, she found me suitable and appealing.

Some of the audience noticed me deliberately ignoring the freak punk rocker and making subtle advances towards Kate.

Myself, a military hero in my own right and Kate, a beautiful actress, started the rumors flying as our encounter went viral.

When I left the show, the crowd applauded me and I thanked them and shook Bettermen's hand for inviting me on the show.

As I walked away I stated to Kate, "I hope to see you, Kate…I really do."

Kate looked at me as if she was emotionally moved but then dropped her eyes down softly to the left leaving me wondering.

Suddenly, as I drew away Kate bit her lower lip in a sensuous manner and raised her beautiful smiling eyes towards me and stated regarding the Chief of Staff Ball, "Barring any prior modeling engagements that my publicist and sub-publicist haven't informed me about, I'll call you Frank."

As I departed I was left wondering did I really make a dent in Kate or was she just being polite for stage purposes?

Or was it the beginning of a beautiful relationship?

Time will tell.

Shortly after I left, Kate left the studio with her publicist and was met by a screaming uncontrollable crowd. As she signed autographs with her fans and took photos with them, she could see farther down the block, a near stadium size crowd surrounding someone that sounded like a rolling thunderstorm due to their applauding and flash photography.

Kate asked her publicist, "Who is that movie star that is dwarfing my huge crowd?"

Whereby her publicist stated, "Kate, that is the gentleman you just talked to on the Bettermen show.

In my twenty years in show business, Kate, I have never seen crowds that size surrounding a celebrity, its unbelievable…. but he is a international hero now Kate and those are his people who honor and follow him.

That said and a word to the wise, Kate, a relationship with him could definitely accelerate and promote your career to the top for years to come. No doubt about it, Kate, the gods have found favor with you today, so don't waste this opportunity by not pursuing him.

Pursue him at all cost, Kate…even if you have to go to Nebraska and visit him.

Otherwise, as I have been told Kate, other attractive and better positioned women of statue are already seriously considering him!"

Kate pondered what was just told to her as she watched this gentleman from a distance laughing and mingling with the crowd, when she suddenly glanced down at the phone number on the crop dusting card that had been given her.

Chapter 4-The Ball

The day before the ball, Kate called me at the air base; I was surprised to say the least. She was pleasant in her conversation and asked me about what was proper protocol for this event and would an evening dress and heels suffice.

I told her absolutely and with her beauty and grace whatever she wore would suffice…. she chuckled and told me she would pick me up at the base's main gate to avoid any searches and complications.

The next day, "Boot" Hill drove me down to the main gate and we waited for the limo.

"Boot" stated, "Man that girl is hot as Nikki, your doing all right for such a homely looking dude."

I joked and replied, "You know "Boot" how's you and that female hobbit that you met at the gay bar working out?"

We cracked up again where "Boot" replied, "She's the best of the five I dated and she wears shoes too."

"Yah," I replied, "but I hear she's a roofer on the side?"

We broke out in tears and our sides hurt from that joke.

As we started talking about our company commander, I spotted a limo approaching the front gate.

I told "Boot," "Don't wait up for me."

"Boot" teased and stated, "You feel lucky, Frank?"

"I hope to be some day, but for now, this one is a lady and I'll treat her accordingly." I stated.

"Boot" replied "Yah right. I'll see you later. Call me if she throws you out of the car and you have to walk home."

Smiling, I stated, "I will."

As I walked up to the black stretch limo, the limo driver got out, introduced himself and opened the door for me.

As I entered the limo, I became numb. Kate was wearing a tan trench coat, which barely covered her short black dress that exposed her sexy legs and gold high heels.

Her golden hair was radiant and her smiling green eyes captivated me. Her beautiful white teeth complimented her gorgeous smiling pink lips. It looked like she was dressed for the bedroom, which was fine with me.

Oh my, I thought to myself, I was ready to do 10 to 20 years of military hard time in Leavenworth Prison for a taste of her, and it would have been worth it.

No doubt about it, she was a head turner and for sure those generals at the ball would definitely eye fxxx her without question for only a real man understands that natural hunger for them.

Damn was I proud to be with her.

As I looked at her, I stated, "You look beautiful tonight Kate, just gorgeous."

"Thank you," Kate stated, "Am I dressed appropriately?"

"Kate with or without clothes, your dressed appropriately." In a heartbeat I realized that what I was thinking and what I am saying out loud should not be the same.

"Damn it," I said to myself, "I have to quit acting like a fat ass Tommy-boy."

"Well, thank you again." Kate stated, as she gave the limo driver the instructions to the ball.

As we drove to the ball, our conversation took off right away. I found her career as an actress and a model to be intriguing and fascinating. It was refreshing to say the least to hear a different take on life's struggle as compared to my military experience of "high and tight," guns, weapons and planes. Her stories were intriguing and wonderful to hear as she described the glitter of Hollywood and the lights of Broadway.

I was fascinated as she talked about the guerilla-style photographers, known as the paparazzi, who drove her crazy and the perverts trying to grab her ass at her picture signings.

Indeed, she was a brave young lady traveling alone at times with stalkers following her.

Yet, as in all women I dated, as I looked into her magnificent eyes, I sensed a high degree of loneliness. Due to her hectic schedule as a model and actress, a "manly-man" never came for her but rather the "boy-men" and the hair fashioning boys from the gay bars would surround her.

As in the song, There is a Rose in Spanish Harlem, this delicate female beauty was in the mist of a sewer of dykes, transvestites, fags, predators, closet queens and money changers that would always gather around her.

I could sense that the woman within Kate knew what she needed, yet the girl didn't, but it is the woman I have come for and therefore, *I must uproot this rose and take her to place in my garden.*

Maybe, I had a chance…maybe.

Funny though, yet hard to believe, the only question I've ever seriously asked the attractive girls I've dated in the past was if they were lonely.

To my surprise everyone…everyone… said they were lonely despite being, intelligent, attractive and graceful.

I murmured to myself, "Was a good man that hard to find, I thought?"

I wondered then, why all those attractive girls I've dated who I believed would have married me; never said there was anything special about me, except that I was the only "normal" and "real" man that they had ever known.

How can that be?

Though up until now, I never asked myself the question, "Was I that good man?"

I don't know, except to say, I had a strong passion for women and loved their company and what money I did have, I shared with them. I didn't lie and cheat on them and always treated them as a lady, yet the dirt bags seemed to fare better then I did.

Was I that good man, that women wanted and yet I never knew it?

I didn't have an answer for that for only a good woman would know.

At the ball we danced slow and ever so close when the music of Nat King Cole's, Fascination and Stardust played.

I was definitely fascinated how radiant Kate looked which caused me to see stars throughout the entire evening. When I embraced her I could feel her heart beating ever so softly against my chest. There was no doubt about it of all the glamorous women at the ball; I had the most incredible beauty and gracious one in my arms.

All eyes of envy were upon us.

Kate was definitely putting me in the mood for romance, yet I knew Kate had to be treated like a lady for I had visions of a long-term commitment with her. Kate lit up my heart that had been in a lonely state of slumber; she was, "a light in a dark room."

Funny though, when I started falling in love with Kate the whole world looked rosy and I got warm all over as if I drank a couple of shots of brandy back to back. With Kate in my arms I felt so alive as if I was a tender plant sprouting and breaking the soil to bask in the sun for the first time.

My God, I didn't want to let go of her, for just the thought of it left me with a feeling of despair that I would never see her again. I just wanted to fuse her into my body so she could be with me forever.

When I laid my cheek to her cheek, I could smell her wonderful fragrance that radiated out from her body and blonde hair.

"My, oh my," I thought, "Woman's taken from man's rib yet there was genius at work here for I couldn't get enough of her."

I couldn't help but wonder what she thought about me or if I'd ever see her again, especially with her busy worldwide appearances to push her clothing line to nearly all the international shoe and clothing manufacturers in Europe.

I inadvertently softly prayed aloud and asked the God of Heaven to give me this one, if it be his will.

Kate then pulled her head away from mine and looked at me and said, "Did you say something Frank?"

Realizing that I was praying aloud, I looked at her and stated, "No Kate, I was just thinking how wonderful it was to hold a wonderful girl like you in my arms."

She looked at me with those magnificent laughing green eyes and her sensuous pink lips that illuminated her radiant creamy white tanned skin and just smiled at me.

She then placed her head softly against my head as we finished out the dance. The rest of the evening, I embraced her even tighter to my chest and it appeared she welcomed it.

Throughout the evening, generals and members of the Joint Chief of Staff came up to my table and introduced themselves to us. They kept the conversation light, yet encrypted as we discussed "The People's War."

Finally, Kate stated, "Frank, I don't know anything about military matters but these high ranking military personnel seem to go out of their way to talk to you.

Just what do you do, Frank, besides being a jet ace and a ballplayer?"

I just looked at Kate, smiled, picked up her tender hands and kissed them, then put them back down on the table and said nothing.

Kate, just looked at me, read between the lines and let it go.

As the evening closed Kate and I left in the limousine, yet all the way we discussed her lifestyle of which I never tired of listening too. No doubt about it Kate loved her profession and enjoyed what she was doing.

As we arrived at the base, I told Kate that sometime I'd love to show her around the base and the planes that I fly.

Surprisingly, Kate responded, "I'd love to see the planes you fly, could we do it now, if it's not a problem?"

"Sure," I said, "However I need to clear you and the chauffer before you enter the restricted area."

After I cleared them through the Marine Corporal at the gate I had the Corporal call ahead to the hanger informing them that I would be coming with a guest.

The Marine Corporal, saluted me and stated, "Your good to go, Captain, their expecting you."

I saluted him and we headed to the aircraft hanger. At the hanger, the chauffer stayed with the limo and I walked Kate inside. There were eight Marines guarding the hanger at the cardinal points on the compass.

As we walked by a Navy Blue Angel F-18 Hornet, I helped Kate up the ladder to the cockpit.

I then asked her, "Would you like to sit in the cockpit Kate?"

She smiled at me with eager anticipation, like a kid going on her first plane ride and stated, "Can I, Frank?"

A naughty humorous thought flashed in my head thinking I got something else you can sit on Kate, but I kept a poker face and stated, "Of course you can, Kate, but with your high heels and short dress, I'll have to pick you up and place you in the cockpit."

Kate looked at me, and innocently smiled and said, "Okay."

So I picked her up and her short dress practically went back to her belly button. Damn, were her long legs tender and silky.

I was afraid, the rise she gave me was showing…but it wasn't, though I couldn't help but think of "Boot's" chubby chewing through a chain link fence.

As I explained to her the characteristics of the plane and how it flew she was impressed with it, but then asked, "Is this the plane you fly, Frank?"

"No," I stated, "I fly the silver one over there, Kate."

So I picked her up again, tenderly grabbing her thighs. Man I didn't want to let go. She was worth going to prison for.

As we walked over to my craft, we entered through the bottom of it; Kate sat besides me in one of the seats and looked curious.

Kate stated, "Frank, how come there's no wings on this plane and it smells like a garden plant?"

I responded, "Kate, it's not a plane?"

Kate then stated, "Frank, your plane, if I can call it that, seems alive and is breathing?"

I looked at Kate's confused face, but had to level with her. "Kate, the craft is alive and you are correct, it is breathing. This craft is not made but <u>grown organically</u>.

Only primitive's societies <u>build</u> vehicles, Kate. <u>In my society we grow every vehicle organically.</u>

<u>That is, our vehicles are living entities, that can repair, feed and heal itself.</u>

<u>Much as a driver is to a car, your soul is to your body, we are to our craft.</u>

I hope I explained that as clearly as possible to your understanding Kate?"

Kate just looked at me and hesitated before asking the next question, "Frank, is this what I think it is?"

As I looked at Kate, she for the first time looked serious, so I stated, "What do you think it is Kate?"

Kate turned and looked at the craft then looked at me smiling, "Frank, is this a UFO?"

I replied, "Kate it's not unidentifiable for we call it "SAVE US" for <u>Strategic Attack Vehicle Earth-United States</u>.

"Is this a flying saucer then?" Now bewildered, asked Kate.

"Ahh…. you could call it that, Kate," as I admired her attractive blonde hair, which complimented her tan complexion, while wishing I could take her up in this vehicle to a quiet place, where I could make love to her.

Kate still looking at me and smiling like an innocent school girl, while not wishing to create a scene asked, "Frank, I knew you were different from the start, just who are you and what really do you do?"

I smiled at Kate, put my arm around her waist and stated, "I can't at the moment say anything more then the fact that I am an astronaut with a rank higher then captain, Kate."

Kate looked at me, smiled and stated, "I know, you're a spaceman, aren't you?"

I said nothing as I softly embraced her and putting my head against hers, as the smell of her perfume intoxicated me beyond measure.

I stated to her, "I am more then just a spaceman, Kate."

Kate just looked at me and said nothing, but intuitively from a genetic perspective I felt, she knew.

Everything about this woman electrified me; I wanted to share my dreams with her so our hearts could beat as one forever.

No more love on the run.

As this enchanted evening came to a close I thanked Kate for a wonderful time.

We then walked back to her limo where I told her it was a honor to be with her and hopefully I didn't bore her too much.

Kate stated she had a good time at the ball and that she enjoyed my company and thanked me for showing her what I flew.

As I opened the limo door for her, I held her hand and told if she ever had any free time from her modeling and acting career to give me a call for I'd love to take her out again if she wouldn't mind.

Kate smiled at me and stated, "We'll see, Frank?" as her window rolled up as the limo drove away.

As I stood out in the dark beneath the stars, I looked out into the heavens. My god, I felt empty as soon as Kate left. I hate living and dreaming alone. Only a woman could fill this emptiness within my heart and provide me the physical and spiritual food that I need.

As I walked back to the Bachelor Officers Quarters, I realized that despite the fame of baseball and flying, I was still empty and hungry.

Only Kate and Nikki have ever come close to filling this emptiness, yet realistically thinking I knew I might never see either one of them again.

At that time I decided to go to the bar and see if "Boot" or "Hitman" were there for a little conversation.

Chapter 5 -The Emmys

As the days passed while flying with the squadron, Kate called me and asked if I would be interested in going to the Emmy's with her and her two girlfriends.

Kate informed me that the Emmy's were about presenting annual awards, by the Academy of Television, Arts and Sciences, to honorees for outstanding achievements in television.

I said I'd love to and if her girlfriends wanted company, I'd bring my buddies, Lt. Jimmy "Hit Man" Calloway and Lt. Billy "Boot" Hill.

Kate laughed and said that would be fine for she had seen my buddies before and found them to be attractive and acceptable.

I laughed and stated, "I don't know if I would go that far, Kate, but what could I do with two bone dead coyote ugly buddies that I found at a rescue mission."

Kate laughed and stated, "Did you ever wonder Frank what they must say about you?"

Laughing, I said, "Well I heard them say many times that women say I'm tall, dark and handsome and women just drool over me."

Kate shot back laughing, "Is that drool over you or throw up on you?"

"Oh my," I said, "You do have a bite."

Kate replied, "Only to those on high horses."

"Kate?" I stated, "I was only joking."

Kate now laughing, "I know. But your not a bad looking guy in any case."

"Thanks Kate." I stated. "I was hoping there was something you saw in me that you liked."

Kate hesitated then stated in a serious tone, "There is, otherwise I wouldn't have gone out with you."

"Hmmm." I pondered and said, "Perhaps someday, you will tell me what you like about me, Kate?"

"Maybe some day I will?" Kate responded.

On the day of the Emmys, Kate arrived with her limousine to pick us guys up at the base in our suits. When we entered the limousine Kate's ravishing companions stunned us. As far as I could tell, both "Boot" and "Hit Man" fell in love on the spot as they were introduced to Kate's companions, Sofia Vega, a dark eyed beauty with eyes like a cat and Christina Orangegate, a dazzling hazel eyed blonde.

I said to myself, "Fxxxen A"; we're cooking with extra-virgin olive oil now!"

I laughed when I saw the smiles on my buddy's faces for I knew what they were thinking and it wasn't about going to the Emmy's, that's for sure.

I'm sure by the look on my buddies faces that if they were left to their own desires with their dates, both girls would have been pregnant by morning.

The limousine stopped near the entrance and as we stepped out, I couldn't help but say, "What a rush" as the professional photographers began shooting pictures of us as we walked across the red carpet.

At the Academy of Television, Arts and Sciences, I was amazed at all the statuesque girls "dressed to the nines" who were walking by us. They looked like Roman goddesses wearing exquisite designer dresses in which I could not imagine how much they cost or how they managed to fit into them. It took every bit of restraint for us three fighter pilots from over eyeballing these dolls so as not to upset our dates. Nevertheless, we were among Americas most heavenly dolls that were all in one place, which we found fascinating.

We stood around and watched all the actresses and actors getting their pictures taken while we tuned in to the buzz of people laughing and greeting old friends.

The atmosphere was similar to the old ballpark at Tiger Stadium, which was vibrant and alive with energy.

On the red carpet, the photographers were shooting picture after picture of the girls who immediately started posing with their actress's flare while "strutting their stuff" like wild peacocks in full plume. We all laughed admiring these gals who had their act down pat to a science as if they were up for an Emmy themselves.

It became a captivating evening with the soft warm breeze and palm trees swaying which made us feel nothing less then incredible as we became immersed in a meadow of beautiful human flowers.

As much as us guys loved talking and looking at airplanes, it would have to play second fiddle to the alluring females that strutted among us. We felt like we were in the song, Standing On the Corner, watching all the girls go by and you couldn't blame us for what we were thinking and dreaming about in this sea of females.

Good god, the women here were just gorgeous and smelled so good with their high priced cologne, that it was enough to put any red-blooded man into a hypnotic trance.

No doubt about it, we were strangers in a strange land, but what a land.

Suddenly I realized, that I never inquired from Kate if she or her girlfriends were nominated for some awards. Jesus, I thought to myself am I going to look stupid and unprepared but I had to ask, "Kate, forgive me, for being so thoughtless. Are you or your lady friends up for any awards?"

Kate looked at me and stated, "No, Frank, we girls just wanted to give you and your buddies an inside track into our world of fashion and art."

"Well Kate," as I looked into her enticing eyes, "I am totally impressed."

A charming blonde usher who surely wasn't in this business for a tip, but rather a contact with someone who would be her ticket to stardom seated us.

Sitting three rows back from dead front center wasn't bad either as we each sat with our accompanied date. Shortly, the lights dimmed and the music reached a crescendo awaiting the host to enter on stage.

As we sat there in eager anticipation for the host to enter, the aisle cameraman fixated on our location and started shooting. In a heartbeat, we were televised worldwide and the girls obviously were taking it in stride as the searchlights began drifting across the audience in a big time Hollywood atmosphere.

As the master of ceremony commenced with the show, we found the entertainment to be amusing and interesting for we three gentlemen were totally captivated by all the elegant women present in one place.

As the Emmy's concluded with their pitch and rewards, the girls offered us a tour of the premise and wanted to show us the notorious Green Room where all the producers, actors and actresses cut financial deals with each other.

It sounded like a fun thing to observe but little did we know certain producers already had us in mind and in their gun sights.

As Kate and the girls took us to the Green Room, we walked among some of the best actors and actresses in the arts and motion business industry. They were not to be overshadowed by the best book authors and television producers shaking hands and discussing business, which was a real pleasure to behold as we three pilots absorbed the chatter like a sponge.

While Jimmy, Billy and I were looking at the exclusive spread of food, Kate interrupted us and introduced us three pilots to two well-known movie directors and a big time journalist out of New York.

Kate stated, "Frank, Jim and Billy, I want to introduce to you to the best movie producers in the business. This is Steven Iceberg and Clint Westwood and their journalist/publisher Freddie Thompson."

"How are you," I stated, "it is a pleasure to meet all of you."

As we shook hands, I introduced my friends, "Gentlemen, these are my good friends, Lieutenant Jimmy "Hit Man" Calloway and Lieutenant Billy "Boot" Hill and I am Captain Frank Legion."

Immediately, Freddie jumped in and stated, "My, those are some pretty ominous names, sounds like something out of the Wild West."

Calloway immediately responded, "In a sense it is, these are names we earned in combat where we put to sleep enemy combatants who wouldn't respond to training."

Freddie looked dumbfounded as Billy and I laughed.

"Would you mind if I ask you three a few questions?" Freddie inquired.

I replied, "Ah, that depends Freddie, for we are under military orders regarding certain matters but you can ask away, if you like."

"Thanks, Frank," Freddie stated, "There's some rumors going around that you three are not really fighting in the far east and the planes you shot down are in question."

"How's that Freddie?" Billy asked.

Freddie replied, "Well the talk is that you three have been involved in underwater warfare against an unknown enemy, is there any truth to that?"

Billy replied, "Freddie, we can neither confirm or deny that."

Kate looked at me and realized we were delving into areas that we were uncomfortable with, so she stated, "Frank, we girls, are going to the ladies room to freshen up and we will be back in a few."

I looked at Kate and thanked her for her keen observation as they left.

Freddie then stated, "There are other rumors floating around that you three are not humans or from Earth?"

Billy replied, "Well, the last time I checked Freddie, none of us are little green men."

We all started laughing.

Freddie asked, "What I mean is, despite the sarcasm, that the human race is involved in warfare off planet and you three are from a distinct race, similar to us humans yet different. If that makes any sense?"

Jimmy swiftly responded, "Your reaching, Freddie boy."

"Hey, I am only stating the rumors, so don't kill the messenger." Freddie stated.

Billy replied, "In warfare the messenger is sometimes killed so he cannot deliver the message to the enemy."

Freddie looked at Billy and stated, "Do you perceive me as an enemy?"

Billy shot back in a sarcastic tone, "You tell us, Freddie. Your standing pretty close to us right now and I believe your stepping on our toes."

Freddie shot back, "Well, I am a journalist and this is what I do folks, get the facts."

Billy responded, "It seems to me that for some time mainstream media and the press has been compromised and you people say and print what you are instructed to say and print. In your own words, Freddie, don't kill the messenger."

Freddie responded, "Hmmm, I didn't think you people were this thin skinned?"

Billy shot back, "We are not and I didn't think you would be this irresponsible?"

"Gentlemen, okay, okay, I get the drift," Freddie stated. "Frank, can I ask you a question, before Billy bites my head off?"

I stated, "You can, but maybe you should take one step farther back and cut your losses and as we pilots say, "depart the pattern."

"Just say, yes or no Frank, then I'll shut up," Freddie asked, "There is another rumor going around that you are in fact a general, Frank, and not a captain.

Moreover, you are an astronaut of some sort and that there is a war in space which you are involved in. Is there any truth to that, Frank? Just asking?"

I responded, "I can neither confirm or deny your question, Freddie."

Jimmy jumped in, "Hey look Freddie, if you want answers to certain questions why don't you check in with Naval Intelligence for answers, if you have the clearances. Otherwise, just ask us mundane questions like how bad is our golf game or questions about the weather."

"Okay, I'll cut my losses for now and lick my wounds." Freddie answered.

"Thanks Freddie." Jimmy answered.

As the girls returned, Kate asked me how things were going?

I stated, "Fine, but we have not had an opportunity to talk to Steven and Clint yet."

At this time, both Steven and Clint who were waiting with patience for Freddie to end his interrogation of us, almost in unison jumped into the fray with questions.

Steven asked, "Frank, regarding the courageous endeavor of you three pilots in the Far East Theater Campaign, "The People's War", as it is called, I was thinking if you three would like to do a movie cinema regarding your experiences with my motion picture studio?"

As both Billy and Jimmy looked at me inquisitively, yet nodded in the affirmative, I replied, "Well, Steven for the moment I will say that's fine as long as the military is portrayed in a positive light and there is no violation of Naval Intelligence directives."

"Of course." Steven replied.

"What will be the name of the movie?" Billy asked.

Steven replied, "I was thinking of naming it "Mig Alley."

We all nodded in the affirmative.

Billy stated, as he looked at us, "That will work, when do we start and who pays."

Steven then replied, "Good, my agent will be in contact with you three with the details for your review in the upcoming days."

As I started laughing, "That's fine, you mean we are going to be professional actors now?"

Jimmy responded, "I'll take some hot blondes instead of payment."

We all laughed.

Clint then jumped in and stated, "Hell, if you make a movie with me, I'll provide the hot blondes free of charge with coffee."

Jimmy then asked, "Are you asking us to make a movie also, Clint?"

Clint replied, "Indeed, I am, but my good friend, Steven, beat me to the draw. So would you three be interested in making a second movie?"

As Billy looked at Jimmy and me stating, "Sure, as long as the same stipulations apply as they do for Mig Alley."

"Absolutely, a contract can be drawn up to those specifications." Clint replied, "I was thinking of naming the movie, "Aces High," what do you think?"

We looked at each other for the moment and stated that the title sounded good.

Clint finished the conversation by also stating that his agent would be in touch with us.

Shortly thereafter, Clint and Steven left and thanked us for our time and that their agents would be in touch shortly.

The girls asked if we were up for a late complimentary dinner in the Green Room, where we all wholeheartedly agreed that it would be most welcome.

During the nice dinner with wine, soft music and light dancing, we all got to know each other better and discussed about meeting again.

We guys all agreed that these girls were hot and keepers, the kind you take home to momma.

We finished this enchanted evening with the hopes that we could all do this again for surely this was a match made in heaven.

Chapter 6-Crop Duster

As the weeks passed, Jimmy, Billy and myself were ordered to Southern California for tactical combat training over the Mojave Desert. We were flying our Strategic Attack Vehicles ("SAVE US") out of Area-51, against the finest U.S. Air Force F-22 Raptors pilots in mock aerial combat. Despite the F-22 Raptor being the best fighter aircraft over the skies of earth it was no match for the Anunnaki-human hybrid "SAVE US" flying saucers. Some of the Air Force personnel were startled to see the "SAVE US" saucer ship vehicles up close and at that moment realized that U.F.O.'s really do exist.

During my time away and until I got reassigned back east, I heard no news from Kate or Nikki from Naval Intelligence regarding matters with the United States Space command.

So, with my scheduled upcoming vacation, I decided to head over to Rick's Crop Dusting Service in Nebraska for a little old fashion flying for rest and recuperation. It was there that I could practice my artistic skills in the ancient art of skywriting, by writing love letters not in the sand but in the sky for lovesick lovers.

Sometimes I would fill the sky full of love letters of which everyone at the Farington Air Field below who was watching got a kick out of.

But I'd tell no one that I was that lovesick fool, though I suspected everyone knew.

Despite all this I hoped the hope of the hopeless that those love letters would stay together and the winds aloft would carry them over Kate wherever she may be.

I guess I had it bad.

The 1928 all yellow Stearman two-seater biplane we were flying here, was especially fun to fly in the morning. During the engine run up period I would rev up the engine, which would cut the early morning dew by creating a milky white vortex over the tips of my wings and propeller as it blew over my canopy. The smell of the farmland and fresh air with geese flying formation below my plane captivated me. My flying and baseball were the love of my life and I couldn't imagine any other type of work, yet as full as my heart felt, I still felt a hunger for something that was missing.

The hunger was not money or fame, nor was it power, but a realization what my heart was truly missing, was a real live flesh and blood female. Without a female of my own and despite the sky being blue or the sun shining full strength, it was still raining and stormy before my very eyes.

With my military vacation leave coming to a close within a few days, I began cleaning up the hanger for my departure. My flight mechanic, Vinnie, challenged me to a game of poker for quarters, so we played cards on the Stearmans wing while drinking beer when suddenly the hanger phone rang.

Vinnie picked up the phone and stated, "Hello, Rick's Crop Dusting Service, Vinnie speaking."

Kate stated, "Yes, this is Kate Winely, perhaps you can help me. I'm looking for a Captain Frank Legion, whom I understand flies out of your flight service. Would you know where he is? I would appreciate it if you could help me."

Vinnie replied, "Sure I can help you, Kate, that big ugly guy is sitting right next to me and he is eating my sandwich and cheating at cards. By the way, he owns this Chapter 11 flight service, not me."

Kate not knowing if she was suppose to laugh or question what Vinnie meant said nothing.

Vinnie came back, "I was only joking Kate except for the ugly part, here's Frank."

"You asshole," I said to Vinnie jokingly.

"Hi Kate, how are you? I'm glad that you called." I stated.

Kate replied. "Frank, I am not far from your crop dusting service and I have my two nephews with me. Is that deal still on for a ride? I apologize for dropping in on you like this and not telling you about coming but it was one of those things that I had to do at the spur of the moment."

"No, there's no problem at all." I said, "But I am happily surprised that you're here."

"Thank you, Frank." Kate stated. "Plus I need to talk to you about something important."

"Fine," I said, "I'll take you up for a flight and my flight mechanic, Vinnie, will take your two nephews up while we talk over a pop and sandwich. How's that Kate?"

"That's great Frank, you're so considerate and accommodating." Said Kate. "I'll be there shortly."

"Swell, I will be waiting." I said.

Within a half hour, Kate showed up in a brand-new silver Porsche convertible with her two nephews, Jimmy and Joey, two thirteen year old blond headed twins.

As Kate stepped out of her car in a short yellow summer dress with white topped toed high heels, it was enough to make my heart stop.

Why is it, as I looked at Kate's long shapely figure that I lose track of time and space and go into some sort of dream sequence, just short of an out of body experience every time I look at her.

I muttered to myself, "Damn, females are beautiful and for the greater part wonderful to have around. They definitely fill the empty void in a man's heart and soul just by their mere presence."

The thought of possibly living this life without a soul mate terrified me to the bone. For what is life without a wife and children but an empty chalice.

As Kate walked up to me, I could hear Vinnie mumble under his breath, "Oh, my God, how did you land something like that Frank?"

I stated, "I haven't yet Vinnie, but I hope to, soon."

"Well, good luck on that, my man." Vinnie replied.

As Kate approached me, she put her arms around me and gave me a sweet kiss on my lips. Damn, for about thirty seconds, I was numb.

"Well, how are you honey?" I asked.

Kate stated, "I am fine Frank."

As Kate looked over to her two nephews stating, "These are my two nephews from my older sister. Their thirteen-year-old twins named Jimmy and Joey.

It takes a while before you can tell them apart, but after a while you get it down."

"How's that Kate?" I inquired.

Kate said laughing, "Joey has freckles and dimples while Jimmy does not."

"Oh, well until I can definitely see the difference, Kate, I will just call them both "Jimmy-Joe" for now, as I shook both of their hands.

"Kate, this is my good friend, Vinnie, former Vietnam combat pilot buddy of mine who is my manager of this flight service." I stated.

Kate responded. "Well, how are you, Vinnie, it is a pleasure to meet you?"

"The pleasure is mine, Kate," stated Vinnie.

I stated, "How about me taking you up in that biplane parked over there Kate? Then Vinnie will take the boys up for a ride after we are done.

Later, I'll cook up some grilled hot dogs, corn, pork and beans on that 55-gallon drum that Vinnie calls a barbecue. Then when we are finished with that I'll show you around the place."

"That sounds great," stated Kate, "When do we start?"

I stated, "Right now if you like? The bathroom and showers are behind you if you or the boys need to freshen up?"

"As soon as I clean up Frank, I'll be ready to go," Kate responded.

As Vinnie showed the two boys around the hanger, I took Kate to the flight line and showed her the 1928 Stearman.

I stated to Kate, "Honey, are you going to fly in that dress, it does get a bit breezy up there?"

Kate replied laughing, "Whose going to be looking at my legs if you're in the front seat and I'm in the back?"

I laughed and replied, "I didn't think I was that obvious, Kate? But in my younger days they use to call me "Gumby Guppy" when I was a kid. That is, my neck could dislocate and stretch a foot or two depending on the need. That said I feel the need for two feet."

Kate got close to me and looked into my eyes and asked, "Do I turn you on Frank, in a big or little way?"

"Kate, you are just drop dead gorgeous to me honey, and you know it," as I looked into her bewitching green eyes.

"Well, thank you for the compliment Frank, am I going to affect your flying capabilities?" Kate stated smiling.

"No, not at all, but my blood boils and I get very hungry when I look at you Kate. There are certain body parts that I have that are overheating and jumping off their engine mounts right about now, Kate." I laughingly replied.

"Should I cool your blood and feed your hunger Frank?" Kate replied in a serious sensual tone as she looked into my eyes again for a hint.

As we just stared at each other for a moment, I replied, "Is this heaven?"

Kate just looked at me as she stepped up on the wing of the Stearman.

"Damn it," I said to myself, "Why, didn't I say.... or take her in the back room... damn it to hell, I blew it."

As Kate stood on the wing bewildered how she was going to step into the rear seat without showing more of her wares, she looked at me and stated, "Frank how do I get in this contraption without making a scene or a fool of myself?"

I then walked up to Kate, put my arms around her and gently lifted her up and placed her with her lovely silky legs in the rear cockpit.

"There, that was easy." I said.

The fun part came when I had to place the parachute harness belt around her breast and then place my arms down between her legs to grab the flight harness and tighten it around her thighs.

I couldn't help but smile as she looked at me inquisitively as if I was discreetly squeezing her charms. By the look on Kate's face she thought I set her up for some free feels.

I did!

I then stated, "Kate, your strapped in real snug and in military lingo, "Your good to go."

I got up in the front seat and told Vinnie to pull the chocks from the wheels as I started up the high performance radial engine.

After the engine run up, I gave Vinnie the thumbs up while Kate waved to the twins.

As I lined up on the runway at the numbers, I went to full throttle with maximum brakes applied as the high-speed propeller compressed the air into a milky white air stream, which blew over the cockpit. I popped the brakes at full throttle and roared down the runway. At liftoff I broke the pattern and headed into the blue, which was laced with cotton ball cumulus clouds at about three thousand feet with ceiling and visibility unlimited.

Talking to Kate over the intercom she stated the climb up was exhilarating.

As I reached the cumulus clouds, I would do doughnuts around them then go through them for an added kick. In the distance I pointed out to Kate a squall line with thick gray clouds pouring rain on the cornfields. Kate got a kick looking down over the cows and pigs in the farmlands. The running of horses that were alarmed by the engine amused us as I circled over their heads.

I then peeled off, down to just over the treetops and headed for an opening to follow a long meandering river. Below the trees now, and skimming the water, I headed for a waterfall that dipped at a juncture point of an adjoining river.

At the falls, I dipped down through the whispery white moist mist and picked up white caps and kayakers fighting the current. Despite their immediate challenges that the kayakers were facing they still found time to wave at Kate and I. I could hear Kate laughing and yelling at them through the intercom.

Kate's biggest kick came as I headed towards a high bridge expansion crossing over the river. I nosed the plane down skimming the water and shot right under the expansion bridge between the support pillars then nosed up the biplane into a high-speed power on stall by rolling the craft into a half-S-maneuver. As the plane shot up, sputtered and stalled, I rolled it to the right and rolled over into a power on dive and shot right under the bridge heading back for home.

I called Kate over the intercom and asked if she was okay, or if she was blowing chips on her dress? Surprisingly, she stated she was fine and that we needed to do this more often, which was fine with me.

As I climbed to altitude, I called Cleveland Center for a straight approach to the airfield and informed Vinnie that I was heading in and to take up the boys when I landed.

Vinnie came back and affirmed my message and stated the kids were anxiously waiting and were so hungry he already fed them a couple dogs, chips and soda.

I thanked Vinnie; intuitively knowing he did this to give me more time with Kate once on the ground.

As I approached the airfield, I called out the approach to final and hit the runway numbers smack on. Pulling up to the hanger to park, Kate could see her nephews waving while anxiously awaiting their turn.

With the tire chocks in place, Kate and I returned back to the hanger for some lunch and talk.

As we walked back to the hanger, Vinnie yelled out, "How did you like the ride, Kate?"

Kate replied, "I loved every minute of it. I can't wait to do it again."

Vinnie refueled the plane and took the boys out for their turn, as Kate and I waved them off.

As I started cooking up some hotdogs with fried onions and beans, Kate put out the plates and garnish.

As we sat down to eat and talk, I sensed a degree of sadness in Kate's face.

So I asked her, "What's wrong Kate? Are the hotdogs that bad?"

Kate looked back at me with a half smile, "No, Frank, the dogs and food are fine."

"Well, what's wrong, you look perplexed." I inquired.

"Frank, I don't know how to say this but there is something I need to tell you about." Kate grimly responded.

"Oh…Oh. I said. "I knew things were too good to be true. Okay Kate, what's on your mind?"

As Kate put down the hotdog, "Well…ah, Frank."

"Just spit it out Kate," I stated, "I am a big boy and I can handle it, so cut to the chase."

"Well, cutting to the chase Frank," as Kate looked sadly into my eyes.

"Yes?" I said, "Go ahead Kate."

"Frank, there is another man. I am secretly engaged to another man, Mike Mountain and I plan on marrying him soon." Kate stated firmly.

Taken aback, I dropped my dog on the plate and stated inquisitively, "Oh?"

Kate then stated, "I am sorry, I didn't inform you of this Frank. I am further sorry, I misled you, I didn't mean too. I never had any intention to hurt you, Frank, for I care about you deeply."

Still stunned and thinking to myself if I cannot mate with Kate then the human species is terminated or at least in great peril of becoming extinct.

Moreover, under the rules of marital engagement for species procreation, I cannot force a selected woman to love me or kill her spouse to be. For if I alter the natural course of events I will be subject to the death penalty by the Supreme Council. For if the woman cannot see the better of the two men or what "being" has the most genetically advance genes to improve probability of survival through intelligence, then the woman is "naturally defective" and should not be the original "Eve" of a species.

Regardless of the rules as things now stand I have failed my critical mission and my right to rule will be critically scrutinized and condemned.

As I shook my head and dejectedly looked at the floor I said to myself how could I have fought all those battles and go through them nearly unscathed emotionally, yet this woman, has just broken my heart and I feel like I want to throw up or cry.

"Damn it," I said. "Is that how it is Kate?"

Kate softly responded, "Yes, that's how it is Frank."

"What does this mean Kate? Are you telling me it is over? Why did you drive all this way just to tell me this? It just doesn't make sense, Kate." I sadly asked.

Kate responded, "What it means is that I am going to marry this man, Frank. I would rather have you and me remain good friends rather then say it is over.

I drove all this way to tell you, Frank, face to face, for my boyfriend, Mike Mountain, didn't want me to see you ever again, but I couldn't leave you hanging because you were too sweet of a person.

Mike Mountain and I got in an argument over this matter but I insisted and decided to tell you face to face, Frank."

I pulled a bottle of whiskey from the cupboard and without a glass gulped down a shot or two in front of Kate. As I sat down and took another gulp of whiskey, I said. "Kate, I'd offer you a drink but I have a strong suspicion I am going to need this whole bottle for myself today, Kate. I apologize for my bad manners."

"That's okay, Frank," as Kate sat on the edge of the table. "I knew it wasn't going to be easy."

I looked at Kate and stated inquisitively, "Marry him? Damn, you just broke my heart, Kate, I wish I never heard this.

You say you want us to remain friends, when I thought we were getting serious…how can I do this, Kate? Jesus….I feel sick at heart."

"I am sorry Frank, I was hoping that you wouldn't take it this bad.", stated Kate.

"Kate," I stated, "You are a special person both to me and my race."

Kate asked, "Race?"

I looked at her and stated, "Never mind."

Kate responded, "Your very special to me Frank. I hope we can remain good friends?"

"Let me see if I understand this right, Kate?" as I looked at her. "You want me to remain a good friend? Hmmm…hedging your bet Kate incase things don't work out?

Is that what's this is about?"

Kate now mad stated, "Of course not Frank, I don't play men…okay. I was at least hoping you would wish me the best?"

"Oh, I wish you the best Kate. Furthermore, I hope your mountain man jumps off a cliff." I sarcastically replied.

"Frank," as Kate looked at me with compassion, "I am sorry."

"Yah," looking down at the ground, "I should have known…"

Kate just looked at me and said nothing.

Shaking my head, I stated softly as I looked straight into Kate's hypnotic eyes and stated, "I don't know what in the hell, the Supreme Council from the Great Hall of my people was thinking about Kate. I don't know how they are going to take this."

Kate looked at me confused, "I'm sorry, what was that you stated, Frank?"

I dropped my head to the ground and stated, "Nothing Kate...nothing at all."

As we sat there for a moment not saying anything, Vinnie and the twins came into the hanger and were talking and laughing about the flight.

The twins were overjoyed which brought a smile to both Kate's and my face as we talked to them about their flying adventure.

Kate looked at Vinnie and me and thanked us for our hospitality.

Vinnie stated, "Your leaving already Kate, heck, I thought you and the boys were going to make a day of this?"

Kate smiled and replied, "I would love to Vinnie but I really must get the boys back home."

After a small chat Kate and the boys left for home.

After Vinnie and I waved them off, Vinnie looked at me and stated, "What's wrong partner? When I took the boys up you looked all bubbly and aglow and when I returned you looked like someone just cut your heart out?"

"Was I that obvious partner?" shaking my head.

"Yes," Vinnie said, it was that obvious. "What happened? Did you get in an argument or something?"

I looked at Vinnie and stated, "Worse, Vinnie, she is marrying another man. She came down here for the sole purpose of telling me that."

"Damn, no wonder!" Vinnie stated, "What in the hell is the Supreme Council going to say? You better get Tron and Omega here ASAP because your hide could be in serious trouble."

"I know." As I looked at Vinnie, "A mission failure like this could mean the death penalty for me."

"But it is not your fault at all, Frank." Vinnie stated.

I looked at Vinnie somberly and stated, "The Supreme Council vehemently hates failed missions whatever the reason. They especially despise race propagation failure for planet seeding purposes.

I worry about a failed mission for the directive of engagement with *"the daughters of men"* by the High Council, cannot be violated.

For there is a belief known to us by the ancient ones of old that without natural love and affection between two people during copulation that their offspring's soul *if conceived out of lust or violence will carry "original sin" and will not derive from the light of high heaven but rather be drawn from the "dark side."*

That soul encased with "original sin" from a lower level of animal and species will be damned from the onset and contaminated throughout its existence as a deviant and wicked soul.

Its only salvation for redemption is the shedding of innocent blood.

At this time I called Tron and Omega to me via the universal organic Vril transmitter to respond.

As soon as Tron and Omega received the message they responded from the Far East Theater and appeared within the hour via their Om transporter.

When they arrived we all sat down and discussed my critical problem.

The Mars Way-Station was notified to inform the High Council of the situation.

Within the hour, the Vril transmitter came alive, cracking with orders from the High Council informing my support units and me to stay on planet Earth until the situation could be rectified.

The High Council further instructed us that we were to stay until the Giants or the upcoming natural calamity either destroyed the earth or if the battle for earth is lost to the Giganthepitechus.

Simply stating, the High Council decreed that I must find out the true nature of the Giants motive on the moon. For our race, the Anunnaki race, wanted to know if there was a new player in our solar system that we would have to contend with in the not to distant future. For we did not know if the Giants true intention was in fact mining the moon or were they contemplating invasion of Earth and other planets within the solar system.

In closing, the message stated, "Hold until relieved!"

"Damn," I said to Tron and Omega. "Protocol forbids me from killing Kate's mate on penalty of death, so that's out of the question.

The Giants are on the moon, motive uncertain.

The Giganthepitechus are inbound with a war fleet to take back the earth.

Natural disaster could occur at any time to the planet Earth and destroy it as it did in the days of Noah.

And here I am on a critical mission to take a selected woman to procreate a new species and preserve genetics of an old species only to find myself with this "daughter of man" who has taken up with another man that appears to be a momma's boy or girl man."

Vinnie, looked at me and started laughing, "I got a bad feeling about all this Frank!"

I said, "No shit."

We both laughed.

Tron stated, "Our intelligence informs us Kate's fiancée left his wife of two years for Kate. It appears Captain that Mike Mountain is an opportunist and a player of women for his own advancement and greed."

Omega then stated, "Seeing Captain, that your orders, "Hold until relieved" most probably means stay until the end, whatever the end may be. I would suggest waiting out Kate's and Mike Mountains relationship which hopefully will fall through before they get married, or they will get divorced shortly after marriage which will provide you another opportunity to win Kate's heart."

"Gentlemen, I appreciate your responses," as I looked down at the ground then lifting my head while calculating a diminished probability of success and stating, "I cannot believe how life is held in such a precarious balance and on such slender threads.

I mean imagine a whole race existence has been put in danger or may fail to occur because some lazy half-man is in it for the money and placing the whole human race in jeopardy.

I guess I'll have to wait it out as long as possible and try somehow to win Kate back."

Chapter 7- Reflections

As the weeks past, I was beside myself like a schoolboy trying to carry books for a girl that refused my advances.

Despite all the activity of the war in space disguised as "The People's War" in the Far East, Kate gone and an "Aces High" movie to make, I still felt very helpless and worthless.

I tried to call Nikki and have her stop by but she was tied up still taking care of her mother or debriefing pilots from the Naval Intelligence Space Command.

Throughout it all I would spend a lot of time reflecting on the matters of earth, "the daughters of men" and the Anunnaki.

I couldn't help but think as God looked down upon the earth upon my works beneath the scorching sun saying, "Vanity of vanities. All is vanity."

As I reflected on the works of men, I marveled at how hard they try to create robots to do functions for men when in fact what they are trying to obtain yet unbeknown to them is what we the Anunnaki did is right in front of them.

You don't make robots to do human work you dumb down humans to a degree to do robots work and this is precisely what the Giganthopithecus intend to do with the human race if they conquer them.

The human body is nothing more then an organic and self-replicating machine, which is much more complex then any inorganic robot.

Robots have to be made while humans replicate themselves through procreation. Robots have to be cared for while human parents care for their children. Robots have to be maintained while humans feed themselves and raise their offspring. Robots are limited to what they can do while humans can just about do anything and are self-sufficient.

Flying saucers can therefore be compared to humans and robots, for if the flying saucer is alive its creator is advanced and if the flying saucer was made out of metals its creator is less evolved.

<u>True flying saucers are grown and not made. They are grown naturally like mushrooms. All advance races grow their machines organically with the option to procreate itself, maintain itself, heal itself and defend itself.</u>

Suddenly, I returned back through time and space again to my body and my situation.

Despite all my problems, I decided that I must keep myself busy by flying with the squadron, crop dusting and skywriting in order to prevent me from thinking of Kate and Nikki.

Many a time I would sit on the flight line alone and watch high performance T-28B's with their powerful radial engines doing touch and goes or taking my Stearman biplane for a ride which would further cause me to reflect on the matters of men.

Then there were times I would just go by myself out in the woods beneath the 200 foot scrub pines to ponder and wonder about life in general. Though at times I would walk out into the meadows and listen to the birds chirping while watching the wheat fields being swayed by the wind gusts that would put me into a hypnotic trance.

It was in this hypnotic trance that visions of yesteryear and the future played out in front of me like holograms dancing before my eyes and I realized that there are so many critical issues I must tell the humans at my first opportunity to do so. This revelation must be told to the human race so as to take away the darkness and the secrecy put in place deliberately by the dark powers that rule this race here on Earth.

Men today are like those during the days of Noah, they could not see the handwriting on the wall, nor see the approaching calamity coming upon the earth, let alone changes in the moon and the sun.

For right in front of men's eyes today the world is changing yet they can only understand the signs of the weather at best but never the signs of the time.

The sun color is changing from yellow to white, which means it is getting hotter. Which in turn means the sun is going from the lower energy infrared spectrum towards the higher energy ultraviolet spectrum.

This means the sun is moving away from amber and between cyan and magenta to become whiter. Which further in turn means the sun is emitting more energy, which means global warming, which means higher sea levels due to melting ice caps in Antarctica, which has become a lake instead of a past frozen ocean.

This also means the ocean conveyor belts are affected due to fresh water icebergs melting because fresh water is less heavy then salt water. This in turn means nuclear winter in certain places, massive super storms and quakes in divers places and followed by three days of darkness as the sun goes from yellow-white to blue black as prophesied, when God of the Universe sends out his angels to gather the weeds to burn them and his elect to place in his barn.

This three days of darkness as foretold in biblical prophecy will be created by a massive planetary object with a diameter of 77,000 miles across which will cross between the Earth and Venus creating a solar eclipse that is a precursor before Nibiru's debris field approaches Earth.

All of this is in front of the human species now, yet they have eyes to see but see not and ears to hear but hear not, just like their ancestors.

In any case only a remnant of humanity will be saved as Noah with his kinsmen were saved from the deluge.

My Great Uncle, Enki, Lord of the Earth, an Anunnaki, spared Noah by allowing him to fill the Ark with certain advance genetic seeds and strains of the earth along with an Anunnaki pilot to guide them to safety on Mt. Ararat.

It was my Great Uncle, Enki, with his advance technology that led the animals in pairs to the boat and not the hand of man.

Moreover, it must be made known upon reflection of Plato's writings that were written by Solon, his grandfather, as told to him by ancient Egyptian priests, from the Dialogue of Critias, which was believed lost, that certain dialogues were altered either deliberately or through misunderstanding.

In truth, the Dialogue of Critias was and has been greatly misunderstood which claimed that the God Zeus created the flood that occurred upon the whole earth.

Yet in fact Zeus, was Enlil, the Anunnaki commander of the Earth and Enki's brother and therefore the corrected version of Plato <u>for the first time known to man should therefore be read this way:</u>

By such reflections and by the continuance in humans of a divine nature (Anunnaki genetic infusion), the qualities which we, (the Anunnaki**),** have described grew and increased among the humans. For many generations, the humans, as long as the divine nature of Anunnaki genes lasted in them the humans were obedient to the laws but when the divine portion (Anunnaki genes) began to fade away, and became diluted too often and too much with the mortal admixture (of human genes) and the human nature got the upper hand, they (the humans) then, being unable to bear their fortune, behaved unseemly, and to (Enlil)-Zeus, (an Anunnaki) who had an eye to see grew visibly debased, for they, the humans, were losing the fairest of their precious gifts **(virtue);** but to those, humans, who had no eye to see the true happiness, they (the humans) appeared glorious and blessed at the very time when they (the humans) were full of avarice and unrighteous power.

Therefore (Enlil)-Zeus, the god of gods, (of the Anunnaki), who rules according to law, and is able to see into such things, perceiving that an honorable race (the humans) was in a woeful plight, and wanting to inflict punishment on them so that they might be chastened and improved, collected all the gods (Anunnaki Supreme Council) into their most holy habitation (The Great Hall), which, being placed in the center of the world (Of Nibiru) beholds all created things. And when he, (Enlil)-Zeus had called them, (the Anunnaki Supreme Council) together, he (Enlil) spoke as follows before the (Anunnaki Supreme Council) members to not tell the human race of the upcoming deluge and let the human race perish.

(Enlil)-Zeus allowed the Earth to be destroyed with it's inhabitants on the close passage of Nibiru when it's gravitational pull would pull the Antarctic ice sheet off it's landmass and into the oceans to flood the earth by raising the sea levels to incredible levels.

Now (Enlil)-Zeus is not God but perceived as God but in fact he is just an Anunnaki commander of Earth yet the God of Heaven who controls the universe and all things seen and unseen including Earth allowed Nibiru to enter into this close proximity with the Earth in order to destroy the wickedness of men, the wickedness of the Giganthopithecus and the original sin of the Anunnaki for mating with lower order human women.

In the Holy Bible, in Genesis, the God of the Universe is confused and used interchangeably with Enlil-god, who is not a god, but an Anunnaki, while the God of the Universe is "One God." And God became the Word. And the Word of God became Flesh and walked among men as Jesus Christ to teach men through his works, teachings and miracles who God is!

That said, the "sons of God" really are the "sons of the Anunnaki's" but the Son of God, is Jesus Christ, God Man and the Holy Spirit.

So my other Great Grandfather, Enlil, Lord of the Command, an Anunnaki, wanted to leave humankind perish for they were reverting back to their animalistic hominid state, which is the savage Gigantopithecus, as they are becoming today.

For the admixture of the Anunnaki strain within the humans today is becoming again deluded and like the movie "Charlie" the humans are reverting back to a retarded being with all their savage animal characteristics and instincts.

The best and simplest guide to determine if one is a carrier of the recessive genes of the Gigantopithecus and is regressing genetically back to a hominid is if one commits sexual acts against nature!

As I continued to reflect I would think about creation of the Anunnaki, the Humans and the Gigantopithecus and wonder how it could come to this.

For indeed it is true, the future is unwritten.

As I stared up into the heavens at the moon, I wondered who were these immense Giants that were 26 miles tall in statue with 178-mile long scout ships hiding in the southern quadrant of the moon. Furthermore they were the advanced guard for their mother ships that are hundreds of thousands of miles across that were hidden in the rings of Saturn for unknown reasons that now were approaching Earth carrying thousands of these beings.

For what?

What is their purpose?

Though I prayed for the best, I could only think the worst.

How would this all end, I wondered?

But what perplexed me the most was, that the whole human race's chance of procreation to a higher level between Kate and I appears will not take place.

For this woman, Kate, a chosen woman, went off with a momma's boy, a ladder climber, who dumped his ex-wife for Kate's money.

Incredible, to say the least how the destiny of the many is held by the few!

Time is so critical now and here I am with nothing, sitting in the middle of nowhere between somewhere and elsewhere.

I lost Kate, perhaps forever…a failed mission, a most definite disqualifier for a king in waiting.

Now Nikki, this gorgeous sweetheart, an ex-nun, who is to be my concubine if Kate cannot produce offspring, won't marry me either because of her sick mother she is tending too.

I can only say to the God of Heaven, how can I overcome this crucial predicament against your unstoppable timetable of change and fulfill the mission of my people and the Supreme Council?

How?

Here I am, a prince, destined to be king of Nibiru and the Anunnaki people, who could have my pick of nearly any female on Nibiru, if I so desired, cannot even keep and hold a "daughter of men."

When I finally do happen to fall in love with a "daughter of men," a woman of my choice that has the approval of the Supreme Council from the Great Hall of my people she decides to dump me for a half-man hobbit from pagan Hollywood.

As I continued looking up into the heavens, I shook my head in rejection and said to myself that there's not a damn thing I can do about this situation but wait it out and hope for a sea change.

The Giaganthopithecus, the Yeti and Sasquatch that are being seen in the remote areas of the world today are in fact the advance recon force for the invasion of earth who are relaying back critical infrastructure information.

They are preparing and gathering intelligence for the main invasion force of the Gigantopithecus.

But this end game will be much different then in the days of Noah. For in those days just before the deluge occurred it was decreed by the Supreme Council from the

Great Hall of my people that only those Anunnaki on Earth with at least 75% Anunnaki genetics could return to Nibiru.

Those with only 65% Anunnaki genetics were allowed to travel to the Mars Way Station, the Moon and the outer planets.

While those with less then 65% were told to fend for themselves and seek refuge in the inner earth at the poles, the ocean deep and the area around Baalbek, Lebanon.

As for the humans, Enlil-Zeus-Jupiter decreed that all should perish.

Nibiru and it's moons are known as the destroyer to the people of ancient times for upon its proximity to the earth it causes great upheaval and turns the earth upside down.

When did this happen...you say?

Yet, is it not written in your Holy Book, "Behold the Lord maketh the earth empty, and maketh it waste, a desolation and turneth it upside down and scattereth the inhabitants thereof.

The earth also is defiled under the inhabitants thereof; because they have transgressed the laws, changed the ordinance, broken the everlasting covenant. Therefore hath the curse devoured the earth, and they that dwell therein are desolate: therefore the inhabitants of the earth are burned, and few men left." Isaiah: 24

In the days before Noah, the human race enjoyed a greater and longer life span nearing 1,000 years due to our Anunnaki genetics within their blood.

But after the flood, the world changed and the human species lost their age longevity because the greater majority of Anunnaki males were not mating with the "daughters of men" for they have left the Earth for Nibiru, Mars, the Moon and the outer planets, taking their women with them to procreate.

In addition to the Anunnaki departure atmospheric conditions upon the earth change drastically after the deluge further reducing the human life span.

During the time of the flood the atmospheric pressure lessened which made humans smaller. Those Anunnaki's who were still on Earth went within the earth or to the ocean bottom to increase the pressure.

Furthermore, the intensity of the sun was greater in the infrared and ultraviolet spectrum due to the atmosphere weakening. This in turn caused aging to increase dramatically upon the human inhabitants who resided on the surface of the planet.

Oxygen levels dropped considerably affecting brain development and reducing mental capacity, which created a state of human global amnesia. The humans could not remember after a few generations on what had occurred to them for none now lived who could remember it and the rest refused to accept the very concept of a worldwide flood.

Humans lost the ability to slow down the aging process when they lost the ability to hibernate, which caused their bodies to burn out quicker.

Chapter 8-Aces High

Throughout the following days, during breaks from the squadron, I along with Lt. "Boot" Hill and Lt. "Hitman" Calloway began going over the script for "Aces High" because "Mig Alley" was delayed due to budget restraints.

The only stress reliever I had was flying my biplane that helped take my mind off of losing Kate and Nikki to her mother.

An acting career didn't appear to be all that bad at times which helped fill the cracks in my armor by temporarily learning a new art that was intriguing.

I never saw so many heart stopping girls all in one place shopping on Sunset Strip.

Yet, there was not a drop to drink….for I had no girl.

For the moment though I found acting to be an endeavor worth pursuing seeing that my baseball career was on hold and my kingship on Nibiru was in question from the High Council due to pending mission directive failures.

I mean the only endeavor I had left was acting though I didn't feel I was the type to play pretend, as actors and actresses always do. For actors and actresses lived in a world of make-believe seen through rose-colored glasses, while my world was just plain gruesome without the frills and in real time.

Thinking that all my life the battles I have fought on Nibiru and the Mars Way Station were for real and to the death in real time. I couldn't help but think the battles fought on the out planets and Mar's moons, Phobos and Deimos, where thousands of humans and Anunnaki died fighting side by side against a superior force of Gigantopithecus, was anything but pretend.

Nevertheless, the producer, Clint Westwood, portrayed "The People's War" in the Far East Theater by attempting to render a correct version through the movie, "Aces High", of what was allegedly happening in that war.

At times on the movie set, I would just step outside for a breather and stand there looking up towards the heavens thinking how I couldn't tell the human race that in the last three months of fighting in space, I, Captain Frank Legion, lost nine hundred and ninety-four pilots, with only Lt. Hill, Lt. Calloway, myself and three other survivors were all that made it.

I couldn't tell the Hollywood crowd or these shapely long legged female actresses that were walking all around me that the battle for space and the outer planets was lost.

I couldn't tell anyone but my assigned Naval Intelligent Officer Nikki, who decided to go home to take care of her dying mother knowing soon the inhabitants of the earth, would have to face the music.

For she knew we lost hundreds of thousands of men and women of Russian and Chinese heritage in space just in the last three months alone who were fighting alongside the American pilots.

I, Frank Legion, as their general, lost them…all of them!

We couldn't hide the fact of such enormous losses of Russian and Chinese people any longer, from even their closed public society.

As I drifted back to reality with my private thoughts I look at these fair-haired female beauties that walked all around me as I was studying my movie manuscript and realized that I couldn't tell them that in a short period of time they will be fighting for their very existence here on terra firma.

For the battle of earth and man's supremacy to rule here was being challenged by the Gigantopithecus and what was left of our mortally wounded remnant fleet, our last bastion of defense, from across the solar system were retreating to the earth. Hundreds of thousands of our ships scattered across the solar system, some on fire, were carrying our dead and wounded soldiers inbound to our last defense perimeter… Earth!

Just as baby sea turtles who hatch on the sandy beaches of the Galapagos's Islands in the South Pacific get picked off one by one by devouring seagulls stalking them overhead as the baby's run for their life, so was our fleet running from the Giganthepitecus.

The Giganthepitecus made it perfectly clear to the governments of the earth and to the Great Hall of my people on Nibiru that from the gaseous giants of Jupiter and Saturn and its rings to the sun belonged to the Giganthepitecus who we believed were attempting to rule the solar system one planet at a time.

They would take no prisoners, nor negotiate for it was a war of annihilation and extermination of species.

It was Stalingrad in space, scorched earth, and no prisoners.

Mankind's last stand was like the Alamo for there was no place to run to after earth.

The battle for island earth, this jeweled orb that floats through the void of space, has begun.

Winner takes all!

It is here on earth that the Anunnaki and the Humans would have to fight and die side by side, as in days gone by, against a tactically superior invader.

It is here on earth where the humans must stand or be exterminated or enslaved to the last man, woman and child.

Then, as sworn by the Giganthepitechus, they will come in their own good time for Nibiru and destroy the Anunnaki for creating this hybrid-mutant species known as Man.

Lt. Calloway and Lt. Hill along with myself knew firsthand as we reviewed our movie manuscript, that this movie, "Aces High", as intriguing as it was, was just a propaganda movie for the Defense Department.

The Defense Department, as it has done in all wars in the past withheld the truth from the masses, glorified the primitive and obsolete art of war to prepare and indoctrinate the masses for this battle to come.

As the movie production continued the directors and producers informed us that each one of us "Aces" had female actresses to play as our wives. Lt. Calloway got Sofia Vega the dark eyed beauty with eyes like a cat, while Lt. Hill got Christina Orangegate, a fiery hazel eyed blonde, and as luck would have it, the uninformed producer thinking he was doing me a good deed, a favor mind you, had Kate as my wife in the movie.

Needless to say I was speechless when I found this out since Kate apparently didn't want to inform me of this matter, out of fear that I would drop out altogether from the movie and severing her lifelong dream for an Oscar for best actress.

My trying moment came in the film when I had to hold Kate in my arms and embrace her….I almost couldn't do it. The love scenes that followed pushed me to the brink for I had to shut down my pheromones completely. Yet, all during the movie production I could not feel the warmth or presence of any of Kate's pheromones…she went cold on me…like I wasn't even there.

I thought of just walking out on the producer and director and telling Kate, I could give a rat's ass about the movie or her winning an Oscar.

Suddenly, reality hit me and I realized that my life was unimportant for the fate of the Anunnaki and human civilization lay in my hands. For as in the movie "High Noon" a showdown was coming. Humanity and the destruction of the earth with the approaching Gigantopithecus fleet were imminent so I forced myself to take Kate out of my mind and heart.

With a broken and heavy heart I did just this, yet the emptiness and loneliness would never leave me.

For what is man without a wife and children?

For I felt whatever love Kate had for me now was gone because when I held her and kissed her during the movie "takes" it was like holding and embracing a cold lifeless mannequin…. it broke my heart.

Throughout our hectic schedule that followed between flying and the movie production, I was heartbroken and lonely. Better stated I was empty, adrift and crushed, yet I hid it well before the producers and director.

I never was a drinking man yet I needed an escape and the only other option available to me was to get drunk in the arms of another woman.

Throughout my life I was told this that only a woman can take away the blues caused by another woman.

Nikki was my answer and after a busy day on the set I would call her and tell her how much I missed her. Yet, her undying love for her mother held me in stasis.

As the weeks followed and the movie reached completion we awaited the reviews with eager anticipation from Hollywood and the press corp.

When finally, the much-awaited news came in…first a trickle, then an avalanche of good news from across the country that the movie, "Aces High" was projected to be a box office smash and had "the right stuff" for an academy award for best picture.

The icing on the cake came when I heard that Kate and I were both nominated for best actor and actress. This good news, which was incredible at the time, made me fill ecstatic and took away my troubles by lifting my spirits considerably.

Moreover, both "Hitman" and "Boot" were both told that they would be nominated for best supporting actors, which would be an understatement to say that we felt less then fantastic.

Against this backdrop, "Hitman" and "Boot" laughed and drank with me on the movie set until the wee hours of the morning wondering how in the hell three clueless actors like us could had pulled this off.

But we did!

We enjoyed the limelight of Hollywood and the neon lights of Broadway by meeting all the various actors and actresses at all the high society parties, which we found to be intriguing and entertaining.

I was always amused when I walked incognito down the main drag of Broadway and Hollywood and stopped at the newsstands to laugh at seeing my face on the front cover of Vogue and numerous other magazines.

This notoriety in turn brought the babes that swarmed us as if we were queen bees of a bee colony; all of them were ripe and ready for spawning.

Indeed we got drunk on their nectar for I drifted through the arms of endless women who were so "hot" that I lost track of time and space and remained in this heavenly bliss, I prayed forever, in the arms of *"The Daughters of Men."*

The Oscars were coming up and all of us were excited of the possibility that the movie, "Aces High" had according to Las Vegas oddsmaker a 3 to 1 chance of winning best movie.

Prior to the day of the Oscars, my buddies and I got ready in case we got lucky and won the awards. Both "Boot" and "Hitman" brought dates that had bit parts in the movie, "Aces High."

Obviously I couldn't take Kate so I dated a young attractive lady that a screenwriter introduced me to on the set.

I seen her around the movie set a few times and her well defined sculpted face and figure was hard to overlook. She was a tall and slender green-eyed blonde who was struggling to be an actress.

My God was she stunning, for I forgot about time and space when I looked into her eyes which reminded me of Anne Francis in the movie "Forbidden Planet."

Yet her demeanor was educated and graceful which resembled the actress Grace Kelly with Jimmy Stewart in the movie "Rear Window."

I mean she was drop dead gorgeous and I thought how captivating women are before men and how defenseless we are in their presence.

Women meant so much to me for I always enjoyed and loved to be around them, especially those that I loved.

Women are a natural seduction of men who become helpless in their arms and what is life without them but an empty cold existence.

She said her name was, Oceania, which was befitting to her beauty.

On the day of the Oscars, our dates were leaning all over us and giving all their acquaintances those phony Hollywood kisses. We made our way through the maze of paparazzi's and photographers from the newspapers and magazines in Vogue that were shooting nonstop pictures of us quicker then automatic fire from a machine gun.

During the course of events, just before the honor commencement by the master of ceremony, Kate walked up to me with her half man in tow and stated, "How are you doing Frank? I just wanted to wish you the best and hope you get selected for best actor."

I looked at Kate and stated, "I'm doing fine Kate and hopefully you are doing well? Don't worry about me winning any Oscars; I'm not a professional actor as you are. I hope for you that your lifelong dream of winning the academy award for best actress comes true."

"Well, thank you" Kate stated, "I see you have a charming date with you, she looks familiar?"

I responded, "Oh, I'm sorry…. Kate this is Oceania; she is my lovely date for the evening. She worked on the movie set and had a minor role in the film."

"Oh really?" Kate inquisitively replied. "It is my pleasure to meet you, Oceania, and I wish you the best in your career."

Oceania graciously responded as the lady she was, "Well, thank you and the best to you tonight, Kate. I hope your dreams will be fulfilled tonight by coming true."

The atmosphere of the Oscars was majestic and magnetic like "electrum" of gold and silver as was the capstone placed on the Great Pyramid by my Great Uncle Enki, an Anunnaki, and the Father of Noah.

You could feel the magnetism in the air, as you walked on the red carpet with palm trees gently swaying in the soft summer breeze. While along the path of stars were giant gold Oscars staring into space as if they were statues from the Luxor Temple on the holy highway in Egypt.

As we walked along, the hum of the crowd sounded as if we were in a bee colony serenading a queen, I mean it was buzzing.

All eyes were upon me and my accompanied drop dead gorgeous beauty, Oceania, as they gazed at this green eyed blonde beauty with legs up to here that swayed alongside me with such precision and grace as that of a queen.

The rumor was, that this raving beauty, Oceania, was in the company of a strange man from Mars, a "Klattu", from the movie, "The Day the Earth Stood Still" while my two seven foot giants "Gort's", named Tron and Omega walked close behind me scanning the crowd for life forms of questionable nature and purpose.

The eyes of the crowd gazed at me with such curiosity and wondered if I, Frank Legion, a soon to be warrior king on the planet Nibiru was their first extraterrestrial contact.

As they looked upon me, I could sense and feel their thoughts that they felt I wasn't human but rather some type of living "being" from an unknown location that looked Homo sapiens like them. As they continued their stare they questioned my motives and why now to their accompanied guest whispering with endless questions.

"What is he?"

"What's his story?"

"Are the rumors true?"

"Why is he here?"

"What does he want and is he hostile?"

"What is that gorgeous date of his doing with him?"

Throughout the whole enchanted evening when the lights dimmed I could see hundreds of eyes in the darkness staring at me as if they were formless ghosts looking at me, probing me with hostile eyes.

Soon, I thought, the people of the earth must be told what is approaching them and their slim to no odds of surviving these events as it was in the dreadful days of the deluge and Noah.

Despite all of the distractions all around me, one look at Oceania settled my uneasiness and I felt good and downright righteous.

As this memorable captivating evening played out, I sat in awe watching the faces of the nervous nominee's anticipation wondering if they would be chosen for an award.

I, myself, never gave it a second thought nor considered the possibility that the movie "Aces High" or me would be nominated.

Suddenly, the announcer stated, "The award for best movie for the cinema industry for the year goes too…………………………."

My heart did stop for a second as I got caught up in the moment when Oceania began squeezing my hand to the point of cutting off my circulation.

"Too………………………."Aces High!" said the host announcer.

As I tried to digest on what was just said I looked at, Oceania, with an inquisitive look and stated, "What, what did he say Oceania?"

Oceania jumped up crying and laughing for joy as she hugged me to the point of nearly passing out.

"Your movie, "Aces High" won, Frank!" as Oceania continued crying tears of joy as she flooded me with kisses.

"Well, I'll be damned," I said, as I looked at "Hitman" and "Boot" jumping for joy about three rows back with their dates, while the producer, Clint Westwood, walking down the aisle waved to all of us to follow him as he called out, "Rally on me, men. Rally on me."

Kate was in tears crying as she stood up to join us as her half man started kissing her lips…. the bastard!

As we all walked up on stage Kate came over and gave me a passionate kiss that reminded me of old times. "Boot" and "Hitman" were just laughing their ass off apparently believing they pulled off the biggest heist of the century.

As I stood there on stage with all smiles and with Kate's arm around me, I realized as I looked out into this wealthy and powerful audience that someday, I would have to make my speech before an audience such as this in which the whole world would be watching.

One speech, one audience, one message about the end of days!

As the night continued the nomination for best supporting actor went to "Boot" and "Hitman" who looked like they were dying from laugher as if they pulled another heist.

They were given a standing ovation as I signaled them with a carrier pilot's thumbs up and salute.

When the award for best actress came up, Oceania leaned over and stated, "I hope your girlfriend wins, Frank."

I looked into Oceania's green cat eyes and stated, "She's not my girlfriend anymore Oceania…you are…if you'll have me?"

Oceania smiled and leaned over and gently kissed me on my cheek stating; "I'd love to have you as my steady, Frank."

I looked at her and smiled, "Good, thanks baby, now were steady."

The master of ceremony then stated, "The award for best actress goes too………."

I said to Oceania, "Why do they have to do this, this suspense will give somebody a heart attack."

She just laughed as she hugged my arm tighter.

The master of ceremony finished stating, "Too Denise Bartlett in the movie, "Saving Miss Guppy."

I looked down at Kate; she was stunned and looked dejected despite her best attempt to cover it.

"Oh my," as I stated to Oceania, "Kate's going to be down for weeks on this one."

Oceania felt sad for Kate and stated, "Maybe she will win next year, Frank, God willing."

I looked at Oceania and stated, "That's nice of you to think like that sweetheart but there is no next year!"

Oceania looked at me curiously stating, "That sounded so final Frank, why is that?"

I looked deeply into Oceania eyes and stated in encrypted format, "On Mars there are no Oscars and Emmy's as you shall see also!"

Oceania looked at me in deep thought and decided to say nothing more.

Finally, the moment came when the best actor award was being presented.

No doubt about it my stomach was jittery but I carried no unrealistic expectation of winning anything, hell, I didn't even have a speech prepared.

Oceania looked at me and stated, "This is your moment Frank, are you ready?"

I looked back at Oceania and stated, "Honey, you being with me is my moment and more important then the Oscar."

"Oh my," Oceania smiled at me and stated, "Now, you're the sweetheart, Frank."

As the spotlights scanned across the audience, the host announcer stated, "And the winner for best actor goes too....................

Oceania squeezed my hand tightly.

"Too..................Frank Legion in "Aces High."

"Oh my God," I said as Oceania gave me the best kiss of my life.

Oceania broke into tears and stood up applauding me as the audience rose to their feet to give this "Man from space" a warm and welcome reception.

Stunned and looking at Oceania, I stated, "Oceania, come up there with me, I don't know what to say or who to thank."

Oceania started laughing, "Frank, get up, it's your moment. Give it your best shot."

As I stood up and acknowledged the crowd, I kissed Oceania and headed towards the stage. I could hear "Boot" and "Hitman" cat calling to me, which got me laughing.

As I walked up on stage and accepted the Oscar for best actor, I looked down at Kate in the first row and she was crying tears of joy for me and waved. But her half man gave me the evil eye. Screw him.

"Ladies and Gentlemen, I want to thank you for this distinguished award from the motion picture industry and I want to thank the producer Clint Westwood and the lovely Kate Winely and my two dear friends and their dates, my comrades in arms, Lt. Jimmy "Hit Man" Calloway and Lt. Billy "Boot" Hill for helping me win this distinguished award.

Thank all of you again for your kindness, your professionalism for granting me the opportunity to win this award. Thank You."

As I walked off the stage, I cannot say how moved I was when the whole audience stood up again and gave me a standing ovation.

Afterwards, we all went out for dinner and celebrated our awards at the best Hollywood parties.

As the weeks passed, Oceania had to return to the stage for minor movie roles in Europe, it was her chance but I was sad to see her go.

I was pretty much left alone and despite having this gold Oscar on my mantle, I would have preferred Oceania, Nikki or Kate at my side now.

I hated being alone.

I overcame my loneliness by accepting numerous invitations to private celebrity functions and mainstream media shows where women were hanging all over me.

The Broadway shows, the lights of Hollywood and the red carpets, celebrity "A" status, the screaming crowds of women mesmerized me.

This celebrity "A" status sure took my eyes and heart off of Oceania, Nikki and Kate especially when I was invited to the private parties. My God, earth women are delightful; I was in a trance for weeks.

Like the song said, "She so fine there's no telling where the money went."

And I don't know where all the money went and I didn't care either, but oh my, the memories.

The hell with getting drunk in the arms of just one woman, I got drunk with desire in the arms of many women. Oh my, it was a women's smorgasbord....I feasted on their honey filling my hearts desire.

The babes, the skirts, the legs, the cologne…man was this heaven, I mean, "I was drunk on women."

However, the day finally came, as it always does when I get too happy or silly, when apparently the Gods of Heaven looked down upon my misbehavior and thought a correction of my improper conduct was in order.

Apparently, as I reminisced in hindsight, too much sugar is not good for anyone beyond moderation.

When Oceania returned from Europe, we would head to the outskirts of Hollywood by Ocean View Park for dinner at an open-air restaurant with the fans overhead blowing the soft sea breeze through her long blonde hair. Her hair swayed in the breeze like a gentle wind blowing over the wheat fields of Kansas and her talk, as always, was that of a well-bred lady with upbringing.

While we were sitting there enjoying a glass of wine, discussing her future acting career during casual conversation, my classified military phone rang.

As I picked it up, I heard, "Captain Frank Legion, Commander Anthony Patrick here, United States Navy, how are you?"

"Fine, sir." I responded, wondering what this blindsided call was all about?

The commander stated, "I wanted to congratulate you first on your Oscar award for best actor and best movie, "Aces High" and the excellent reviews Hollywood and Broadway has given it.

I understand you're spending some time on furlough in the Hollywood area, enjoying the sand and surf before you return to the "People's War." Am I correct?"

"Yes, commander, I am, and I have a charming young lady sitting across the table from me enjoying dinner with me. Would you care to join us?"

The commander got the drift immediately and stated, "That's most kind of you captain. I apologize for interfering with you on your private time, so I will make my intrusion brief.

I am in charge of the United States Navy Flight Demonstration Squadron, the Navy Blue Angels.

Recently three of our pilots who were scheduled to fly a scheduled flight air show with us from the Marine Corps Santa Ana Airfield unfortunately came down with food poisoning last week and are being hospitalized for a unknown specified period of time."

I replied, "I'm sorry to hear that commander is there anything I can do to help you?"

The commander came back, "As a matter-of-fact there is captain, which is why I am calling you. We have an upcoming high profile flight demonstration show at San Francisco's, Golden Gate Bridge Bay Area next week and we need three pilots ASAP for the United States Navy Fleet Week Demonstration.

We understand the Secretary of the Navy and perhaps the President of the United States will be present aboard the nuclear aircraft carrier USS Ronald Regan which will be anchored near the Golden Gate Bridge area.

I understand your friends Lieutenant Jimmy Calloway and Lieutenant Billy Hill along with yourself are carrier qualified in F-18 Hornets which is what we are flying here.

Cutting to the chase captain, is there anyway that I can take you three men away from your private time and get you to fly the demonstration next week with the team?"

I responded, "Of course, commander, Lieutenant Calloway and Lieutenant Hill have been assigned to me for some time now and we will leave tomorrow morning and be ready to go by first light."

The commander happily responded, "Thank you captain for your favorable response on such a short notice, I'll be looking forward to meeting you three tomorrow."

"The pleasure is mine commander," As I closed the conversation.

Oceania, sadly looked at me and stated, "Have to go, Frank?"

As I gazed into her aqua green eyes, I thought to myself, I am not walking out on this beauty so I stated, "Not until tomorrow sweetheart. How about I get us a bottle of wine and two glasses and we walk down by the ocean and enjoy the rest of the evening together."

Oceania responded, "I'd love that Frank."

As I looked at her, I stated, "So would I baby, I really enjoy your company and hope to see more of you."

As we got up from the table to walk out, Oceania kissed me on my cheek and stated, "So do I, Frank."

The following day Lt. Calloway and Lt. Hill along with myself saddled up and headed to the San Francisco Bay Area.

When we arrived at the squadron stationed in Santa Ana, California, we were met and greeted by Commander Patrick who informed us that he would take us up to show us the lay of the land and where certain maneuvers would be conducted.

After a three-day briefing, training and computer simulations we all felt we were ready and "Good to Go."

The maneuvers the Blue Angels used were basically tactical maneuvers we used every day in combat against the Gigantopithecus in space and we were in the top of our game on these matters.

The Bay Area was breezy and surreal as we walked up the three step hills on the west side adjacent to the bridge to gaze out into the Pacific Ocean and to discuss our maneuvers. The area was windswept and we could see Alcatraz Prison on the eastern side of the bridge. I couldn't help but think about the movie, "Escape from Alcatraz" and thought it didn't look like that bad a swim at all despite the sharks and myth. "Boot" started joking and saying he could go the distance with backstrokes alone while "Hitman" stated he could make it by just diving off at Alcatraz, the B.S. got so thick I told them that I have to put boots on if I had to listen to them any longer. I told them all things look easy from a distance; nevertheless, they still believed even with a strong current that their excellent conditioning could have made the swim and win the day.

After watching the boat freighters come and go, each heavy laden with their unknown cargo heading to their unknown location we became mesmerized over the fog that swept in from the Pacific Ocean in a heartbeat blocking the enchanting view of the bay and leaving us standing in a fog so thick we couldn't see our noses.

As we waited for the fog to break we headed across the bridge to San Francisco to Fishermen's Wharf to eat at an outside restaurant, "Jimmy's Fish and Crab."

After eating lobster and crab we walked the wharf area amidst a young energetic crowd, which reminded me of baseball. The crowd, the smell of food like cotton candy and the scent of a good burning cigar filled my nostrils. We were amazed at all the sea lions basking in the sun by Pier 39, the "locals" stated at times in the winter there would be near a thousand of them enjoying the sun.

We spent the rest of the day talking about life in general and reviewing safe approaches for the upcoming flight demonstration. We were all pretty excited about flying with the Blue Angels for it was another feather in our hat and a refreshing change of pace.

While we were sitting on the wharf basking in the sun, Nikki called and gave me an update from Naval Intelligence on the "approaching storm", the war in space and the Gigantopihtecus's advancement.

Despite hearing all the bad news it was refreshing to hear from Nikki. Nikki told me that she heard about the situation with Kate and me breaking up and was sorry for me. She asked if there was anything she could do to lift my spirits. I said yes there is and told her to come and stay with me but she laughed and stated besides that.

I couldn't help at that moment to think about Nikki who was a true nun, true to the bone; she wouldn't mess around until she was married. No doubt about it Nikki who had a high percentage of Anunnaki genes in her, was morally and ethically upright and worthy of marriage.

But the laws of the Anunnaki superseded desires and passion for blood precession demanded that the spouse of marriage was the one with the highest percentage of Anunnaki genes and anyone else was to be a concubine.

This is how we preserved our life's longevity of living hundreds of thousands of your earth years. For the higher the human admixture was with Anunnaki blood, the lower the life span of the newborn, plus the inherited human diseases that is a contagion among human beings.

This is why ancient humans had such long life spans and while today's humans are reduced down to three score and ten.

Another part of the problem came when the earth, which in the olden days orbited the sun between Mars and Jupiter until a celestial collision pushed earth into a closer orbit around the sun to where it is now.

The earth's radiation increased due to its closer proximity to the sun reducing human longevity. Atmospheric pressure decreased making humans smaller and decreased their longevity. The oxygen levels changed further decreasing human longevity.

These are the reasons why some Anunnaki who were left behind during the flood due to having too little Anunnaki genetics decided to go underground to the inner earth or the bottom of the ocean.

For by going within the inner earth or to the depth of the ocean it increased the atmospheric pressure as it was on Nibiru, which in turn increased and maintained their life span. The oxygen levels were adjusted to match that on our home planet, Nibiru, in order to maintain our long life span. Lastly, because they went beneath the ocean and within inner earth it reduced the suns radiation levels allowing them to maintain their longevity.

Now you know how, "We," the Anunnaki, have walked among you since the beginning!

However as humans continued mating without injection of Anunnaki blood infusion the humans generics slowly began to revert back to the animal stage from whence they come.

That is, they were becoming more soulless, violent and paganistic like their ancestor the Gigantopithecus.

For this reason in part we, the Anunnaki, have to save the genetically select humans and like God of the Universe bring those select seeds into the next age.

In this case Kate genetically won over Nikki. But Nikki, a carrier of advanced Anunnaki genes, was more then just a beautiful highly evolved human female with a wonderful personality who could naturally win over your heart and soul.

Like Kate, Nikki also was my kind of woman, yet it looks like that I lost both of them.

Nikki then stated she heard I would be flying with the Blue Angels in an upcoming air show in San Francisco's Golden Gate Bay Area and asked me what position I would be flying.

I told her Blue Angels one through four will be flown by Navy and Marine pilots in a four-plane diamond formation. Angels five and six would be flown by Lt. Hill and Lt. Calloway for high altitude and inverted flight maneuvers. As for me, I would be flying the rarely used number seven to "buzz" the crowd on low altitude runs at near the speed of sound over the bay.

Nikki then stated she would be at the air show and was told by Kate and her husband that they would be there also. So in passing Nikki mentioned that I should put on a good show, because Kate stated she would wave to me from the third step hill west of the Golden Gate Bridge as I passed over.

I told Nikki I'd be looking for her on my low level run over the bay.

Nikki closed the conversation on an upbeat note by saying if she can getaway afterwards she'll take me out for dinner and pay.

I was delighted and thanked her but I couldn't help but think that here I am, a prince who may be king someday on the planet Nibiru, ruler over all the Anunnaki people and governor over the earth and the affairs of men yet at best I could barely find a female to go out with me.

I couldn't help but think "What's wrong with this picture?" I mean you would think all the gold digging females that litter the known universe would be swarming all over me? But no, it was like I was invisible and nobody gave a rat's ass who I was or what I was to be.

I might as well have been a hobo with a bottle of suds riding the rails.

Hell, the only date I can now get is with a woman who will buy her own dinner.

Some of us are gentlemen and are looking for a long-term relationship just like they are…enough said as I came back to the world.

The day of the air show came up on us fast as we reviewed all the emergency procedures before maneuvers with all the other pilots. The day was sunny and blue skies, CAVU (Ceiling and Visibility Unlimited); it looked like a perfect day with just light to mild winds out of the Pacific. The crowds were enormous, estimated at two million with many of the spectators lining the Golden Gate Bridge that was closed to traffic. The Bay Area was packed with sailboats and speedboats to watch the show for free.

As we pilots marched abreast onto the flight line so the press photographers could have their day, I could here the narrator Commander Patrick state, "Gentlemen, man your airplanes."

As we climbed into our airplanes each one of us was assisted by the aircraft flight crew chief and made "Good to go." We started up our engines in a billowing cloud of white smoke as if the thunder gods themselves were there in person. After we went through the pre-taxi procedures and engine run up we taxied just short of the active runway. We all gave the thumbs up to Angel One, flight leader that we were ready to roll on him.

The tower replied, "Blue Angels you are cleared to the active runway 22 right, wind two-three-zero at five knots, cleared for takeoff."

Following Angel One we rolled onto the active runway and lined ourselves up.

Angel One acknowledged the tower, "Angel One, roger tower, cleared for takeoff. Light'em up Angels."

We all went to full power simultaneously where Angels One through Angel Four started their roll. As they reached the halfway point down the runway, Angel Five and Angel Six started their roll. As Angels One through Angel Four lifted off and headed into the blue in their diamond formation Angel Five and Angel Six reached the halfway point when I started my roll.

Rolling down the runway at full throttle in the runway markers flashed by me in a moment of time as I watched Angel Five and Angel Six break into the blue and go to full afterburner chasing Angels One through Four. As I cleared the active runway, I went to full afterburner and headed straight up to twenty-five thousand feet in a New York second. I rolled the F-18 on its back and dropped the nose straight down and headed to the earth at 500 mph. As I headed towards the Golden Gate Bridge, I could see Angels One through Four fly over the crowd in their diamond formation. In a moment of time Angels Five and Six came at the crowd from two different directions sending them scurrying in all directions.

As I reached 500 mph from out in the Pacific, I made a head on run between the bridge spans toward Fisherman's Wharf. The crowd was jumping like monkeys as I shot above them upside down between the spans. I mean the place was rocking as I whipped around over the seal pier and headed up to ten thousand feet for another run. As I pulled a hammer head stall, I rolled the F-18 Hornet over on it's side for another run as I watched Angels One through Four do a diamond burst over the bridge sending the crowd into a frenzy. Angels Five and Six came at the crowd again from two different directions and went into a vertical scissors maneuver directly over the crowds at mid-span and headed up to thirty thousand feet.

As I rolled back around, I hit the afterburners and came down over downtown San Francisco between the buildings screaming at 600 miles per hour. We made our presence known both to those civilians at the show and those who forgot to show.

In a flash I busted out over Alcatraz Prison and headed down towards the Golden Gate Bridge and the Pacific Ocean where all the tugboats were shooting their water cannons in the air as if they were German 88mm Flak guns.

As I screamed over the bridge span, with compressed white air rolling off my wings, I could see that the crowd was in a state of total pandemonium who were now climbing all over the bridge's super structure.

The crowd came to party and I wasn't going to let them down.

As I cleared the bridge I shot over the three step hills that was west of it and looked down for a moment where I thought I saw Kate waving.

As I broke out over the Pacific, I went back to full burners and headed skyward to thirty thousand feet. At Angels 30 (30,000 feet), I rolled the F-18 Hornet on her back and headed straight down to the Bay area at 700 miles per hour trailing red marker smoke.

From a distance I could see Angels One through Four do a diamond formation barrel roll right over the bridge followed by Angel Five and Angel Six screaming in, in hot pursuit.

As I rolled down over the Pacific Ocean I got down to tree top level and headed inbound near the speed of sound at mach one like a great white shark heading into a school of fish.

As I screamed towards the bridge at this low height and speed, I created a ground effect at full afterburner leaving a rooster tail behind me over the water. Moving like a bullet between the sailboats and ships that were lined with spectators, I headed for a near supersonic run beneath the bridge for my grand finale with the crowd. With my rooster tail in tow and compressed milky white air all around my jet intakes I could see on the bridge above me the jubilant crowd waving to me as I approached.

I was giving them a memory they would never forget.

As I approached the bridge I could see what appeared to be water bottles falling from the bridge and realized I was in trouble.

Nevertheless, I was committed and had nowhere to turn but go through the debris field and hope for the best.

As I headed under the bridge, I heard a thump then an explosion as my starboard engine exploded and shutdown immediately.

Suddenly, Angel One called out, "Angel Seven, your starboard engine is on fire, EJECT-EJECT!"

I responded, "Affirmative on the engine fire, Angel One, that's a negative on ejection, to close to San Francisco, Fishermen's Wharf Pier. Will attempt turn around...over!"

"Angel Two, tower."

"Tower go ahead, Angel Two."

"Angel Two tower, we have a Mayday in progress. Request runways cleared for emergency and fire trucks with foam dispatched...over."

"Tower, Angel Two, affirmative. Mayday in progress emergency personnel with crash trucks dispatched."

"Angel Two, roger that"

"Angel Three, tower, have rescue choppers dispatched with emergency crew on board."

"Tower, Angel Three, affirmative on emergency Coast Guard Rescue chopper notified and in the air from Santa Ana."

"Angel Three, roger that tower."

"Tower, Captain Vella, Aircraft Carrier Ronald Reagan, cancel Santa Ana, we're here and have three Marine Helo's going airborne with S.E.A.L.S."

"Tower, affirm Reagan on cancellation, you have three choppers going airborne with S.E.A.L.S."

I then jumped in, "Angel Seven, tower, if I can, request straight in approach to runway 22 right. I'll be coming in hot or dead stick over."

"Tower, affirm, Angel Seven, all planes holding short of the active runways. Crash trucks approaching scene."

"Angel Seven...roger that tower."

As I headed over Alcatraz, I banked hard right over Fishermen's Wharf and then downtown San Francisco.

I have to make it to the sea somehow for if I punch out now I may kill hundreds of innocent people.

I couldn't live with that.

Suddenly, my port engine shut down and I was praying that I could at least dead stick it into the bay with minimum casualties. As I banked and climbed for altitude my speed dissipated but I had a chance to eject over Arcatraz.

I attempted to line myself up where there was little to no pleasure crafts...but damn it, they were everywhere!

Suddenly, I heard another thump and fearing the worst, I looked back and there was Lt. "Boot" Hill in Angel Five with his aircraft nose pushing against my aircrafts shutdown engines.

"Angel Five, Angel Seven...I got your back. I'm going to push you out to sea...stay above stall speed."

"Angel Seven to Angel Five, affirm, push to sea...God bless be careful, Angel Five."

Angel Five, true to form and in eighteen wheeler terminology, came back, "That's affirm, good buddy...I'm with you."

As I looked to starboard, Lt. "Hitman" Calloway, in Angel Six rolled up besides me and gave me the thumbs up and I affirmed.

As I rolled down into the bay heading to sea, there was Angels One through Four directly in front of me in diamond formation paving the way beneath the San Francisco Bridge approaching mach one.

All seven of us Blue Angels were screaming over the waterway with rooster tails in tow heading towards the Pacific.

The crowds on the shoreline and the bridge were spellbound and mesmerized as they watched seven fighters in full afterburners with their red smoke tail plumes and water rooster tails roar by them.

As we screamed under the bridge, I suddenly heard another explosion; my aircraft was disintegrating as I screamed out, "Mayday, Mayday…. I'm on fire, going to eject!"

Angel Six broke off and headed to the mainland then Angel Five broke hard left and headed to the island.

Angels One through Four peeled off and climbed for altitude as I headed out to sea alone into an offshore fog that was rolling in.

In my last second of free time I looked at the three step hills with the hope of seeing Kate and Nikki but the danger of the situation immediately drew me back.

As I approached the fog, the fire spread into the cockpit where I ejected out of the burning aircraft engulfed in flames.

As I cleared the flaming aircraft, I looked up as my chute opened and I was horrified to see that it was on fire as I drifted down towards the sea of which I could not see due to the fog.

My hands and flight suit were on fire as I splashed into the Pacific Ocean.

Cutting myself loose from the chute entanglement, I started treading water as the choppers approached.

Two Navy SEALS jumped in the turbulent wake on both sides of me and put me into the rescue hoist that would pull me up to safety because I was choking in the roaring waves of water beneath the chopper's prop wash.

People said later, I looked like a shooting star enveloped on fire when I jettisoned into the fog.

In the days that followed I spent three weeks in the military hospital thinking maybe the gods of heaven had a strange way of getting certain women's attention by having all of them rethink and reprioritize their priorities of what they have and may lose if they continue to play their hands wrong.

"Boot" and "Hitman" who visited me often were told by friends on the scene that Kate collapsed on the ground as I shot by on fire and Nikki fell to her knees crying.

I had a lot of visitors in the weeks that followed, especially Oceania and Kate, who would bring me flowers and candy.

When your sitting in traction with second and third degree burns on a portion of your hands, neck and legs, there was nothing more you could do or say, except to thank the girls and everyone for coming.

I did a lot of soul searching during this time and reevaluated my own priorities and mission in life.

I decided I was determined to fulfill my destiny and to that end I would endeavor until the end of my days.

I realized as I laid in my hospital bed the critical importance of my mission again and come hell or high water, I had to save the human species and my own earthly Anunnaki brothers and sisters, **"The Anon's"**, who are my direct descendants from extinction.

I had to refocus and put all my energies to the defense of the earth and the destruction of this warring savage race the Giganthepitechus who were heading our way and took no prisoners.

During my last day as I lay sleeping in my bed, I was awoken by a soft tender kiss on my lips and the cologne of flowers opened my eyes.

My god, what a beautiful face, is this an angel as those soft brown eyes were looking at me from one inch away. Is this heaven, I thought?

"Hi Nikki, nice of you to come and see me."

Nikki responded, "Hello sweetheart, how are you? I brought you some candy treats."

I said, "I'm getting better Nikki, god you're gorgeous. When I look into your magnificent soft brown eyes that are as gentle looking as a dove, my spirit soars like an eagle."

Nikki started laughing, "I would have been here sooner Frank, but Naval Intelligence couldn't afford to let me go due to unforeseen events in space. So I got here as soon as I could, honey."

I looked at Nikki and asked her, "Is the war in space getting too grim to tell me now Nikki?"

"I didn't want to affect your healing process, Frank." as Nikki looked at my catheter.

"The war is grim, Frank. We tried to negotiate with the Gigantopithecus again, but their answer was simple, "Surrender the earth or we will exterminate every human contagion on it" and as an example they showed us twenty-five of our captured pilots.

They pushed these pilots out into the void of space towards earth from their ships without any space gear on, so they could become meteors as they entered our atmosphere, Frank."

I shook my head, "Fricken savages!"

Nikki stated, "Our fleet can hold them for a while Frank, but day by day it is getting worse. It looks like the planet earth is going to become "The Alamo.""

I grimly looked at Nikki stating, "I know Nikki. I knew it all along. I'll kill as many of those bastards if they try to hurt you, Nikki."

"Oh, what a sweetie. I know you will Frank." Nikki softly smiled and put her nose to mine.

The thought of Nikki, Oceania and Kate dying filled me with rage and sorrow. I was determined to save them to my last dying breath.

As Nikki looked at me she said, "Frank, are those tears in your eyes?"

As I came back to my senses, I said, "No, Nikki....allergies. Where's Tron and Omega?"

Nikki seriously looked at me and stated, "Their down the hall, Frank. Do you want me to get them for you?"

As I leaned up from the bed, "Yes Nikki, would you please?"

"Of course," stated Nikki, "But before I go, I cried when I seen your plane explode Frank and when I seen you eject on fire into that fog. I screamed and fell to my knees. I was told Kate collapsed and was taken to the hospital emergency room after suffering a concussion."

In sadness, I shook my head, "I never meant for any of this to happen Nikki.... I'm so sorry for all this."

As Nikki walked up to me and kissed me on my forehead, my body lit up like a firefly as a lovesick fool that I was. I thanked her for coming as she walked out the door and stated she would see me again soon.

As Tron and Omega walked into my room they crossed their right arm across their heart as a customary salute to their prince.

As I saluted back, I asked, "Tron and Omega, my ancestors thousands of years ago hid three horrible weapons in space never to be used again on each other. They were weapons of mass destruction, planet destroyers. They were hidden somewhere on Nibiru, Mars or Earth.

Contact the Mars Way Station and the Great Council on Nibiru and tell them I want to have them as a last ditch effort if the Gigantopithecus overwhelm us."

Tron asked, "Is it your intentions Captain to use this weapon of annihilation on the earth and destroy all life?"

I seriously looked at Tron and stated, "It is Tron! If we can't have the earth then I'll scorch it, rather then give it to these savages."

Omega replied, "Dead man switch Captain?"

I quickly replied, "Indeed, Omega, the earth belongs to our people and our kingdom...for in the beginning there were wars fought in the heavens.... we won and own the solar system which is contrary to the Gigantopithecus one-sided point of view.

If I am to be king someday over Nibiru plus rule earth and its people justly and compassionately, I do not want to compete with these savages such as the Gigantopithecus."

Tron looked at me and inquisitively asked, "If the Supreme Council says no or if the weapons cannot be found, Captain, what then?"

As I lifted my head from staring at the ground and looked directly into Tron's eyes, I grimly stated, **"Then we will lose the earth!"**

Chapter 9-Bettermen Show

As the weeks and months passed, my health returned to me and I was given a medical up chit to return to flight status and to my squadron for combat flying in the alleged "People's War" in the Far East.

From time to time I would see "Hitman" and "Boot" who kept me abreast of the matters in space. As always the reports and news coming in from space regarding our fleet was going from bad to worse.

I couldn't help but wonder what would become of all this and would I die on earth and be forgotten after the dust settled and somewhere out there someone would find my skull or skeleton and realize that my interior wasn't from earth.

As I thought about my problems in life and space, I couldn't help but think what an old baseball third base coach told me once, "Frank, there are two kinds of people in this world and only two. There are those who don't care about your problems and there are those who are glad you have problems."

I couldn't help but laugh how true and pertinent that statement was on Nibiru, Earth and the Mars Way Station. It must be the way life is across the galaxy, I take it. That is, no one gives a damn about someone's misfortune for they only care about their own little menial personal business until misfortune finds them.

Maybe nothing matters at all and I should just follow the adage that the French have about life, "Give glory to the God of heaven, drink the wine and let the earth be the earth."

I mean whose going to remember me one hundred years from now anyway and what happened in this window of time.

Perhaps I should have my personal scribe, Rasid Anon, who is a direct descendant of the Anunnaki from the "Great Hall" of my people, from the tribe of Anon, transcript the circumstances of this upcoming historic event in case events turn unfavorable, as I suspect they will.

For if I do not do this, as time passes, history will become legend and legend will become myth, for then, none now will live who will remember it.

*Therefore, I must leave a book, a journal behind for the people of the earth must know what was, what is and **what will be**.*

I will name this book, after the beautiful and delightful women of the earth, "The Daughters of Men."

So let it be written, so let it be done!

As I returned back to my reality I realized a vacation was in order.

When my vacation finally did come up I would return to my crop dusting and sky writing flight service for it was the only way I could get my mind on track and my focus back.

One day, as I returned from a sky writing detail and entered the hanger, Vinnie came up to me and stated, "Frank, you had a call from a gentleman who schedules Broadway performances for the Bettermen Show and he wanted you to call him ASAP."

I said, "Is that all he said Vinnie, anything more to it?"

"Well," Vinnie replied, "He just wanted to know if you would be interested in appearing on the Bettermen show?"

"Hmm," I said, "The lights of Broadway and Hollywood are calling me back. Good, maybe the gods have found favor with me again."

Vinnie laughed, "Don't you have enough problems with women, Frank?"

I laughed, "Yah, your right, Vinnie. Along with the war and my kingship too."

Vinnie responded as he put his hand on my shoulder, "Make the call Frank. It might be worthwhile."

"I will Vinnie."

As I walked to the phone I couldn't help but think about Kate and wondered if I would ever see her again. I thought not.

After I talked to the gentlemen from the Bettermen show he asked if I would be interested in appearing on the show the following week. I told him I'd love to and I would do my best to charm Mr. Bettermen and the audience.

When the big day came, I was shocked to find out that Kate was on the show just before my take. Apparently everyone still thought we were still hot and heavy. I didn't want to break the news to the audience differently and make a scene. I hoped Kate wouldn't either and let sleeping dogs lie.

When Kate was finished with her bit she received a standing ovation from the crowd who looked at her as the apple of their eye.

As I watched her from the backstage room's television, I found Kate to be as radiant and beautiful as ever as the first moment I laid eyes on her.

The stage manager then did a slow Texas swagger up to me as I was checking my military uniform for proper alignment, when he called me to the on deck circle.

As Mr. Bettermen made my announcement I walked onto the stage and the crowd also gave me a standing ovation in light of my academy award and aircraft injury. They raised my spirits considerably for one never knows what the crowds are thinking of you beforehand. As I waved to the camera and addressed the crowd I then turned and shook Mr. Bettermen's hand for allowing me on his show again.

I then turned to Kate and apparently she was as nervous as I was about our situation so I kissed her hand, thereby, putting her at ease and asking her with Mr. Bettermen's permission to sit again in the first seat.

"Always a gentlemen." Kate stated.

"Thank you, Kate." I replied.

At this moment in time, Kate and I dropped our defenses or concern regarding our situation and acted like old times by keeping matters light with false smiles.

However, the mood quickly changed from a very joyful mood to a sobering appearance as Bettermen brought up how us "lovebirds" were doing and the subject on where my next tour of duty will be.

I could not believe he did not know about our relationship, but apparently he was uninformed despite numerous magazines stating the contrary.

So I avoided the relationship issue and prayed Kate would dog it too as I jumped right into discussing with him the war in the Far East.

So I told him and the audience that I would be returning to the Far East "Peoples War" to search for two members of my squadron who were shot down by enemy combatants and were believed to be still alive and on the run from captivity. While everyone found this interesting and concerning, Kate suddenly went into a near state of shock on why she was not informed of this matter in private.

Kate looked at me with a serious look and stated, "What…what…you're leaving?"

I stated, "Yes Kate, I have too."

Kate responded, "What about us, Frank?"

"What?" I stated, oh Christ, I thought to myself, here goes, so I replied, "Kate, you know I loved you and yet you have made other plans regarding your future as I have."

Kate angrily repeated, "What about us. You told me in private, Frank, about all those men dying and all those men that were lost that the public doesn't know about.

Why do you have to go back Frank to that war in space?"

I quickly responded as I placed my left hand or Kate's right arm to steady her, "Kate, what I told you in the past was private and classified. You can't say in public what I entrusted you with in confidence. I told you that. You're going to get me court-martialed Kate."

Mr. Bettermen then became alarmed and attempted to jump in and defer the conversation by saying, "Wait a minute, I didn't mean to get us involved in national security matters. Can we start again? I mean C'mon folks, lets be civil."

I shot back, "Was your first wife civil, Mr. Bettermen?"

Bettermen put on a phony laugh but getting my drift, chuckled, "You got me there, Frank."

I looked down at the floor then at Mr. Bettermen and stated, "I'm sorry Mr. Bettermen, my emotions at the moment got the better of me."

Mr. Bettermen smiled and stated, "That's okay, I know the feeling Frank."

Kate, as I figured, wouldn't go away quietly as I turned my face to the audience attempting to pretend and look as if I was in control. But women have a six sense and just don't listen at times as I sat before millions of people trying to keep my cool and avoid conflict.

Yet, I knew in that moment this matter wasn't going to get better for Kate was ready to snap. I then realized that I had to do the unthinkable and just walk off the show before matters go out of control.

My theory was correct, yet it was too little too late.

Kate replied, "Yes, you told me, Frank. Why do you want to give up your life?"

"Kate," I responded, "You're talking about protecting a species…the human species which could be exterminated. Now I have to go."

As Kate grabbed my uniform she stated, "I am not going to let you go Frank, I am not going to die like some old woman after the past wars who died alone.

Someday I am going to look back at this day, Frank, and hate myself for letting go of the only man I ever loved and I let him go to die in some meaningless "People's War" in the Far East.

I'm not going to do it Frank…. I'm not going to let you go."

"Kate," I stated, "You know right now that there is a man out there you are making plans with to marry and another million men out there in the television audience that would love to love a woman like you. You don't have a problem finding a man, Kate.

As for me there is probably not one woman out there that would want to have me despite my position, power and authority. So don't worry, Kate, you can find another man. That said I have to go back, Kate, for the urgency requires it so."

Kate started screaming, "I'm not going to look back and weep all those days saying in my loneliness why did I leave him out of my arms."

I then in anger threw my attached microphone from my lapel to the ground so the audience could not overhear our private conversation.

Kate stated, "What is the meaning of this Frank, I thought we had a meaningful relationship between us? Why are you doing this to me?"

The audience homed in on Kate's personal comment as some female observers in the audience began to cover their mouth in awe, wondering if this was some real life love affair occurring in real time or some domestic violence case that was transpiring before their very eyes as if it was something right out of the soaps.

I mean those in the know, knew, this was front-page news in the making…tabloid news!

I quickly picked up on where this conversation was going so I angrily grabbed Kate's ear microphone and threw it towards the back of her chair thinking it was out of audio range.

Bettermen leaned back in his chair, confused and wondering whether this is some put on act or if in a New York second he would have to call for a commercial break. But in a flash he quickly put two and two together and realized that we two high profile celebrities had been apparently involved in an intimate and romantic affair that may have gone sour.

Kate then starts hysterically crying in full view of everyone.

I said to myself, "Oh…Christ."

Bettermen realizing an uncontrollable scene was about to occur rotated his hand in a circular fashion to the camera crew to run a commercial, in order to avoid further embarrassment.

But it didn't matter for the camera crew standing behind the curtain offstage was videotaping and Kate's microphone was recording our conversation for the world to hear in vivid detail exposing all our dirty laundry.

You know I am a very modest person and I like to keep my personal matters private yet experience has shown me when a female goes off the deep end whether justified or not for they could care less who hears what as long as they can have their say. It reminded me of the old adage, *"Never get in a pissing match with a skunk, for it doesn't mind pissing on you or itself and it doesn't mind the smell."*

Kate then raised her voice while hysterically sobbing, "Frank, how can you do this to me?"

I mean the audience looked at me as if I was some lowdown dog, what was I to do.

"Got to go," I thought, "I can't win this fight, don't want to anyway…. got to go."

I stated to Kate, "Kate, I am a commissioned Marine Officer and I have an obligation to fulfill to God, country and the Marine Corps, okay?"

"You've done your duty," Kate angrily replied, "Your military record confirms it Frank. It's time for someone else to carry the burden."

I looked at Kate as I shrugged my head, "That's not how it works Kate, for *the faith of the few bring salvation to the many,* I have to go and do my duty.

Some of us men act responsible Kate and answer the call to duty. We're not all street pimps or inner city gigolos whose main mission in life is to hustle women, impregnate them, and then dump them?"

"Nonsense," Kate states, "You and I both know that good men like you are just dying for the expansion of corporate America and the New World Order. Nothing more!

Wake up Frank…how dumb are you?"

While Kate was hysterically crying she embraced me and pulled me to her, nose-to-nose and almost lips to lips.

She whispered, "Do you have to go?"

I replied softly, "I must, Kate."

Kate responded, "Someday Frank, I'm going to be an old woman looking back at this moment in my life. Wondering why in heavens name did I let you go from my embrace…. am I too going to be like all those women during wartime that lost the love of their life?"

"Don't say that Kate," as I dropped my head while looking at the floor and shaking it.

"Am I Frank…is that how this ends?" as Kate, sobbing bitterly, looked into my eyes while trying to deny the inevitable.

As her tears of love poured down over her face and nose, she became more radiant then ever…. almost glowing.

I couldn't look at her anymore, nor release her from my embrace; I couldn't let her go; yet I must.

As Kate whispered into my ear she stated, "You're in my arms Frank and I already miss you. Doesn't that mean anything to you…. hmmm?"

I looked at Kate and responded, "I didn't know you cared for me Kate. A girl of your status I felt just hung out with me because you were just being kind…that's it."

"Oh, is that what you thought, Frank…hmmm?" Kate said angrily, "Is that what you thought…answer me damn you. ANSWER ME!"

"Kate," I replied, "Your making a scene honey, we're on T.V., don't do this to us, the audience is staring us down and Bettermen is going to run out of commercials. Try and be civil, will ya?"

"Civil? Is that the word…huh?" Kate angrily replied in a raised voice, "Civil…the man of my life is going to go die and you want me to be…CIVIL!"

As Kate pushed me away from her lips she smacked me with her left hand across my right cheek drawing blood from my lip.

Dodging blows like a boxer in the ring, I stated, "Kate…please…control yourself, will you, I'm practically begging you."

The audience was stunned and realized that this was no act but a real life showdown between lovers in plain view of the audience and our private laundry was being aired.

"Civil…is that what our relationship meant to you…civil?" Kate stated.

As I looked at Kate's crying green eyes that were as magnetic as when she was smiling, "Kate, I sincerely did not think you cared about me. Moreover, I felt in truth you would be glad to get rid of me for I was a nuisance to your busy schedule."

"CARE!" As Kate angrily smacked me for my comment with her right hand across my left cheek and nose.

"Damn you…. you fool." Kate yelled.

As the audience looked at me with concern, I looked back at Kate and stated, "Kate, no more hitting…. that's enough."

"Care about you, you say?" Kate responded, "I don't care about you, Frank!"

Realizing that the crowd had heard Kate's raised voice and that she didn't care about me, I never felt as low in my life as I did that moment for it was even worse then being tagged out at home plate before a crowd of 50,000 spectators.

As I looked back at Kate, I grabbed my Marine Corps raincoat from the couch and stated, "Kate, why did you have to say how you feel about me in the public square and expose our private matters? If you don't care about me Kate, then why are you making such a fuss over me and throwing our personal matters out for the world to review?"

As I attempted to stand up and leave in front of the viewing audience in shame, I felt like a puppy with my tail between my legs, when Kate suddenly grabbed me and pulled me to her. As she placed her lips to mine she whispered, "Frank, I don't just care about you…I'm in love with you."

With a surprised and curious face I looked at her and stated, "What did you just say?"

Kate stated again, "Frank, I'm in love with you. I realize that the phony glamour of Hollywood and Broadway is nothing compared to true love."

As I looked at Kate completely numb…. and speechless. Thinking to myself, what about that loser Mike Mountain? Yet suddenly in one moment of time I was lying on the floor crushed and the very next moment I'm ascending to high heaven, which was tough to adjust to.

Stunned, I replied, "Kate don't do that, don't say that now…. don't lie to me Kate."

Kate looked at me softly and pulled my arms around her and softly pressed her lips to mine and stated loudly, "Now, tell me you don't love me, Frank…. tell me, in front of everyone. Tell me!"

"Kate, I said, "your making a damn fool out of both of us and ruining our careers or what's left of it."

"You know I loved you Kate…more then my life. I have an insatiable desire for you, Kate, which only a natural man has for a natural woman. But you left me for another man, Kate. So, don't shame me now or play me the fool either. Kate, I must go…I must now."

Kate started crying again and passionately replied, "I'm not letting you go Frank, for you're the only natural and real man I have ever known."

I replied, "I am not a man Kate, I am an Anunnaki."

Kate yelled back, "Don't play games with me Frank!"

As I looked at Kate's face, I could not tell the difference if she was sincerely in love with me or she was off her rocker.

Kate then pulled my handkerchief from my rear pocket and wiped the blood from my face and the side of my nose and stated, "Now we are both sissies, for even Marines need a handkerchief," as she wiped the blood from my brow saying, "Your not going to leave me now, are you Frank?"

Then I sadly whispered to Kate, "Yes, I am, but someday I will come back for you, Kate, however long it takes. Wait for me, for I will find you wherever you are…wait for me!

Now listen Kate, a commercial is coming up and it appears by the look on Betterman's face, he is running out of them, so let me leave peacefully."

At this time Bettermen interjected and leaned over his table and softly stated, "Ahh…. guys and dolls, you might want to bring closure to your disagreement, it's my last commercial and we are coming back on the air.

I can't cover you both anymore; you're making a scene on national television. So what you have to do, do quickly and wrap it up!"

As my head swung back from looking at Bettermen to Kate, I replied, "Kate, don't hold me back, if I don't go you and the human race may perish. There are men downed out there who are carrying our battle strategies and tactical battle plans with them, so I must attempt to rescue them.

Besides that, they are my good friends. I just can't leave them to die, Kate, not even for your sacred love."

Kate shot back, "Why does it always have to be you? You've been out there long enough fighting in this secret war; you've been shot down and hurt enough. Why should you always have to go, let someone else answer the call of duty?"

"Kate you know we are losing the war in space, on Mars and the moon. The war for Earth and the survival of the human species is about to begin. Think beyond yourself, Kate."

"I am thinking beyond myself, Frank, I am trying to save a man's life... your life."

"Ahhhh….Kate." Shaking my head, "I can't talk to you when you're like this."

Kate started to cry.

I stated, "Give me a kiss Kate."

"No," Kate angrily stated. "I am not going to give you a last kiss Frank. I am not going to give you a final goodbye either."

As I grabbed my microphone off the floor I then realized as I was speaking to Kate that her microphone that I threw off her ear prior did not clear her as I thought, but had inadvertently got caught in her hair meaning our whole private conversation was aired on national TV. The audience had heard our intimate conversation and the women in the audience were deeply moved with compassion at our state of affairs.

Broken, I stood up, I apologized to Mr. Bettermen, and stated, "I am deeply sorry Mr. Betterman for ruining your show on national television, I truly am."

As I looked at the audience, I stated, "I apologize to all of you also, I am terribly sorry."

It was then that the cameras came back on the air as I walked off the show.

Kate was crying with her head in her hands as if she just heard word of a loved one dying when suddenly the television audience returned back from a commercial break…leaving them to wonder what the hell had just happened when they were away.

For they had seen Kate and me smiling and laughing just before the commercial, now I was gone and Kate was sobbing bitterly with her face in her hands while Bettermen was leaning back in his swivel chair with a thousand yard stare, shaking his head and twirling a pencil wondering what the hell he was going to do next.

And since there was no explanation whatsoever to the television audience the studio phones began ringing off the hook.

Thinking the worse as I left, I felt Kate and I were going to be the laughing stock of the nation.

But little did I know that the gods had found favor with my embarrassed red-blooded face, for red was their favorite color.

The next day almost all the vogue and chic magazines from Broadway to Hollywood across the country carried the story with Kate's and my picture pasted on the cover of their magazine. All the newspapers and tabloid magazines had a special rush on the news even stating the Queen of England had her butler pick up an addition, saying, "Mum's gotta know!"

Unbeknown to Kate and I, we had reached overnight the seldom celebrity status "A-1-Prime" which was top of the heap.

Americans loved us for our vulnerability, passion and openness before their very eyes. The public had an insatiable appetite for more and with eager and restless anxiety wanted to know what was forthcoming.

A real life romance, "A Romeo and Juliet" scenario between a handsome fighter pilot from beyond and a glamorous lady from the glitter of Hollywood and Broadway who were torn between her natural love and his sense of duty while placing all their cards on the table before the world to view without shame.

From uptown to downtown, from Manhattan to the cornfields of Nebraska, Kate and I were the talk of the town!

Chapter 10-The Man in the Moon

The Nielson ratings exploded for Bettermen from one million viewers a day to over five million while the Internet was humming with rumors of our affair as if they were African bees in frenzy.

The women from sea to shining sea were mesmerized and infatuated with our story, a real life love story was unfolding right before their very eyes. Even the soaps ratings across the board had dropped considerably and played second fiddle to our situation.

Whenever I returned from "The Front" and in the presence of Kate, we drew huge crowds as the Nielson ratings continued to soar for any show that presented us together.

From this single event Kate and I ended up on the circuit visiting, "The Bettermen's Show", "The Viewer", "Good Morning American" and the Jay Keno show. The national night shows were the only places Kate and I could meet due to our hectic schedule and flight training.

Producers only wanted us because of the huge increase in their Nielson Ratings and viewing audience, while Kate was playing this for all it's worth.

Kate never felt ashamed for saying that she loved me and she didn't want to lose me to some war she and the rest of the uninformed humanity never truly understood.

I never see Mike Mountain around much anymore but I never probed or built up a false hope but rather just let nature take its course. For I have been a believer that if you play the game of dice long enough, 7 and 11 have to roll sometimes.

Nevertheless, I knew the dire situation I was in and I was under strict orders from the Supreme Council to not meddle in Kate's affair but let her find her own way out and make another selection freely if need be.

But time was ever so short and somewhere out there, they were coming for all of us.

In secret I returned to space undercover of "The People's War" and in the weeks and months that followed I returned back to the moon on a reconnaissance mission to search for my lost friends, Lt. Calloway and Lt. Hill who were shot down while attempting to discover the Gigantopithecus's weaknesses. They were now on the run and carrying our strategic codes and battle plans for defense of the earth.

After desperately searching I found my friends wounded in a cave in the region of Tarus-Littrow Valley, where Apollo 17 astronauts had landed in December 1972 to check out our ancient artifacts in South Massif, which we left behind in days gone by before we created the hybrid man from the Gigantopithecus.

But to my dismay I discovered our strategic maps were lost somewhere on the moon and our only hope was that the Gigantopithecus would not discover them.

During the firefight that ensued to find my friends I suffered second-degree burns again on both my hands from a Gigantopithecus sapper screaming, "Jihad" who was on a suicide mission when he exploded right in front of me.

It was at this time Tron and Omega stated we must get off the moon for the moon was swarming with enemy hostiles both the Gigantopithecus and the Giants of old.

Despite our most gallant efforts to determine the Giant's motives they would only say in their communications to us to stay away from them and their classified mission.

Our intelligence operatives recently discovered that the Giants were created by an unknown advanced intelligence shortly after the big bang of the universe, which was around 14 billion years ago.

Apparently, as best as we could understand it, the Giants were procreating at a phenomenal rate where one Giant would build a factory and make a million replicas of itself then send those million Giants to various moons in the galaxy that orbited planets with advance life forms.

Our best scientist hazard a theory that the Giants may have been created by the Creator of All and that they were replicating and dispatching themselves at the speed of light throughout the universe to prepare for the great harvest at the end of the age.

The Great Council greatly troubled by our losses on the moon, dispatched a message stating to destroy the moon if need be and the Giants included.

I did not want a war on two fronts so I returned dispatched, "Order refused!"

On this order my whole kingdom and my race was at stake and I made a decision that would leave me as an outcast and a leper if the Giants seized the moon, invaded earth and the Mars Way Station.

To make matters worse, I was then advised that Kate did a turn around and married Mike Mountain in a private ceremony.

What treachery I thought, I am out of luck and time, with a superior enemy force closing in on us on all fronts. Women were abandoning me; the Great Council had severely criticized my decisions and leadership abilities while thousands of dead soldiers faces under my command without any victories, haunted me.

Is there hope for the hopeless?

As I returned to earth from the ensuing battle on the moon I was awarded my second congressional medal of honor by the President of the United States though the specific correct details were never revealed to the general public.

As time passed, I pretty much spent my time going over invasion plans for the defense of earth. In my solitude I would stand on the shore of the Pacific Ocean by Crescent City, California staring into the rolling waves of the misty shining sea, knowing that from this direction my annihilated fleet will be returning.

As we waited for the attack, months past without any signs from the Gigantopithecus invasion fleet as I waited to hear the invasion of earth had begun.

Why were they waiting…no one knew.

My celebrity status led me to be invited to so many Hollywood and Broadway social functions that took my mind off of the thoughts of war.

It was at the Fanity Fair Party that I found out the troubling news that Kate already had two children from her boy man, Mike Mountain.

It was then I talked with Tron and Omega and advised them that the Great Council's procreation plans was a total failure and that I now must focus all my moves with Nikki and Oceania who were both high percentage carriers of Anunnaki genes.

I further requested a stealth ship to respond and take any Anunnaki's left on earth, especially the children of Anon, along with precious cargo of any select "daughters of men" to flee to the Jupiter Galilean moon, Europa, where an advance fleet of Anunnaki raiders were cloaked in secret to continue the war.

The High Council further affirmed my concerns and dispatched a reconnaissance fleet from Mercury to position themselves behind a near Venus asteroid and await further instructions for a final rescue or counterattack.

Chapter 11- The Final Play

As the months passed, Nikki finally came back online and informed me what our latest space probes have discovered about the Giants main fleet in the rings of Saturn.

She then told me she had tickets to the Oscars and would I mind attending with her to discuss the secret matters.

I laughed and stated, "Oscars? Nikki, Rome's burning and Nero plays the fiddle."

Nikki replied, "Hardly Frank, there are enemy spies everywhere now and our best intelligence believe there will be no spies at the Oscars."

I replied, "Damn, your right Nikki, who would have thought that the earths strategic battle plans and survival would be discussed in plain view in front of actors and actresses at the Oscars?

If the situation wasn't so serious it would be almost laughable, Nikki?"

Nikki replied, "I know, Frank, but that's how intelligence works by staying hopefully one step ahead of our enemy.

By the way, Frank, the itinerary states Kate will be there."

"Oh?" I questioned.

Nikki responded, "I thought I'd give you some good news and a heads up, Frank."

I replied, "Nikki, that hurt. I never knew you to have a mean streak?"

Nikki responded, "I'd like to think I don't Frank, my intelligence just informed me that Kate is divorced from Mike Mountain.

I thought sweetheart that would be of extreme importance to you?"

I said nothing.

Nikki repeated, "Frank?"

I said nothing.

"Frank are you there?" asked Nikki.

I said nothing.

Nikki thought she heard crying and stated, "Frank answer me. Are you okay? I thought I heard crying?"

I came back on the phone, after clearing my throat and stated, "Marines don't cry, Nikki. I'm not okay.... okay.... and I am not crying.

I just needed a time out."

Nikki replied, "There's nothing wrong with crying and real men do cry.

What I am trying to say, Frank, is that you may now be able to fulfill your prime directive of your mission?"

"As I told Kate. I am not a man, I am an Anunnaki. But thank you anyway Nikki." I then replied, "I know now your just being helpful and thoughtful, Nikki. Now what in the hell am I supposed to do?"

Nikki then firmly stated, "Go get her, Frank!"

"Yes, your right Nikki, I must do that, if she will have me back?" I replied. "It seems Nikki, I live my life on the edge everyday and then every woman I meet gives me the slip."

Nikki laughed.

When the Oscar event came up I picked up Nikki and headed for the presentation. I couldn't help but admire her clean-cut lines and simple but elegant grace. The stunning red dress that covered her hourglass figure and the scent of her perfume was giving me an out of body experience. This dark haired beauty with her cameo complexion and long well-formed legs that were utterly gorgeous in heels was causing my blood to boil.

This doll was a keeper for someone and as selfish and greedy as it sounds, that someone was going to be me.

I couldn't stand the thought of losing this angel to some half-wit closet queen like I did with Kate. Both Nikki and Kate had all the perfect makings of an ideal wife and mother and as a matter of fact so did Oceania.

It was in that moment of time that I transformed from what I was, to what I was destined to be and do.

For the young male in me, finally was overcome by the Anunnaki King within me, which had awakened from its slumber and was filled with a terrible resolve to survive.

Therefore, these women, Kate, Nikki and Oceania, were all coming with me and wherever we are or will be, it will be from there that I'll start this new race along with my other Anunnaki brothers who were assigned this mission.

These three, come either willingly or I take them screaming…*but they were coming with me forever!*

Suddenly like Noah and his family in days gone by, I was the new Noah and life would begin again wherever we were and the only thing that mattered was that we were together.

If Kate was not coming willingly then she was coming against her will. For I decided right then and there that Nikki and Oceania would be my concubine and I was just going to steal all of them if worse got to worse.

They were going to me mine and I would fight to the death and cheat if anyone or anything got in my way.

Simply said, I would bring all my power, authority and intelligence to bear upon any power that opposed me now without mercy.

For I tried to accommodate everyone's wishes as a gentleman and I tried to follow all the rules to a "T" and it just plain didn't work. So it will be done my way where losing and "no" was not an option.

Kate was coming with me with her children and I don't care about any sorry ass excuse she may have.

Further, there would be no more excuses about caring for Nikki's mother which was holding me back for I was taking this sweetheart, this bride of Christ, to be with me forever and she could bring her mother.

As for Oceania, this radiant doll was going to undergo a sudden career change on another planet and like the rest, she will be the mother of my offspring.

The Supreme Council could complain all they want but I refused to spend all my days as a bachelor to dream alone when heaven was right in front of me *if I was bold enough to act.*

And act I did!

To my scribe, Rashid Anon, who has been instructed to write this book, "So let it be written, so let it be done…now and forever, for there will be no failures on my watch…. period!"

The way nature and the wars were going only just a handful of us were going to survive it just like in the days of Noah.

I have to settle down sometime and Kate, Nikki and Oceania was as good as I could get of *"the daughters of men"* in these closing moments of this age.

Therefore, I am going to violate all the Supreme Council's rules and regulations and just plain out steal these women and start my own race if need be.

At the Oscars, Nikki talked with a lot of actresses who were to my surprise covert intelligent operatives looking for cloaked enemy spies that infiltrated this free society.

Nikki told me that those Gigantopithecus children when cleaned up and shaved could pass as humans and that they were and have been walking the earth among us.

I told Nikki that my latest intelligence from the Mars Way Station stated that the recent rash of sightings of Gigantopithecus around the world and especially in North America were not just random hominids wandering around in the deep forests. But rather, they were an advance guard of strategically placed Giganthepitechus conducting reconnaissance of our defenses around the globe.

The people of the earth were not informed of this though for if we made them aware of this there would be mass hysteria, so we let them think they were just stumbling into hominids inadvertently.

As we made our way through the talkative actresses and actors, I noticed not too many journalists or reporters talked to me….I guess I was yesterdays news…a washout.

Well, in some ways that was good news for if they did not know my real mission directive then my secrecy was still being maintained.

At the Oscars we sat down in the third row from the front stage and awaited the presentation to begin when I seen Kate sit down in the first row. Kate glanced at me but when we made eye contact she dropped her lovely eyes and looked sad.

Apparently what Nikki told me was right, Kate was a free lady again and I had to make my move if there was a move left.

During the three-hour ceremony Nikki informed me that the Gigantopithecus fleet was amassing on the dark side of the moon and an attack would now occur within weeks.

I feared that news.

Our combined weakened fleets couldn't hold the line anymore and were ordered from the Great Council to abandon their positions and set up a defensive perimeter above the earth to hold until relieved from the Anunnaki main armada that was inbound if it could arrive in time.

Nikki then hit me with more bad news that our deep space probes and the Anunnaki's monolith on Mars's moon, Phobos, detected a vast armada heading to earth. The ships were of immense size up to 300,000 miles across with "beings" 26 miles tall drafting the Giganthepitechus invasion fleet.

"Oh my God!" I said, "This is it!"

The evidence suggested that the timing was more then coincidental and that this must me a coordinated attack. It appeared to our intelligence divisions as best as could be determined that both races wanted the earth without humans, in a winner take all three-way war.

Again in this moment of time I stepped to the plate and determined that none of these races were taking the earth and I needed a plan.

Our sensors were picking up these Giant's ships approaching which were so massive that they were causing perturbations with the gas giants of our solar system.

Latest intelligence continued to pour in confirming that these Giants are the Giants of old from the creation of the universe and were Angels of the Most High God.

"My God," I thought, "Must I fight God too?"

Our combined intelligence confirmed again that the Giants intention was still not known with certainty so I decided via communications that Nikki would inform the rest of earths intelligence operations to daisy chain all the 24,000 nuclear missiles on the earth together via electronic remote to form a dead man switch for me.

I told Nikki that I would hold the dead man's switch and I would detonate it to destroy the whole earth and its inhabitants if these invading forces attempted to take the earth and enslave its inhabitants.

I will scorch and lay waste the earth and its seven billion inhabitants before seeing this Anunnaki creation fall into the hands of savages or beings with unknown intention.

As I discussed earth's final battle plan with Nikki, I closed the conversation with her by stating in no uncertain terms, "Nikki, you know this horrific event that will be occurring on the earth is an end play, don't you? And you know the consequences if we, the Anunnaki, don't leave with a our designated females, don't you?"

Nikki looked at me with concern and stated, "Of course I do Frank, simply said, we lost and our species is exterminated."

I forcefully said to Nikki, "Your coming with me Nikki and no is not an option, you understand!"

Nikki hesitated, "But.... my mother Frank?"

Angrily I replied, "She's coming too! Nikki, I have given orders to Tron and Omega to take you screaming or kicking...BUT YOUR COMING!"

Nikki started to cry.

I responded, "Cry all you want Nikki, but your coming with me!"

Nikki kept crying.

When the presentation ended we were invited to the best post Oscar party at the mansion of the publisher of Fanity Fair, Mr. Jim Fairweather.

When Nikki and I entered the premise the publisher who reserved a table for us graciously greeted us with his friend, "One Eyed Jack" who was with Kate.

One Eyed Jack started laughing, "Just call me Jack, Frank."

As I looked at Jack, I asked, "Okay...you a poker player?"

Jack stated, "No, I was a pool player back in the day. I used to play at a place called Nick's Pool Hall in a rough and tough neighborhood in southwest Detroit.

I got in a fight with a guy named Bugzy over a game of snooker. He knocked my eye out with a cue stick, which fell on the pool table where he tried to sink it in the side pocket. Can you believe that?"

I didn't know if I should laugh, cry or hold a poker face without bursting into a hysterical laughter.

"Tough love." I replied.

"You bet." Jack stated.

As we sat down, Nikki quickly claimed her red eyes were victim to allergies and asked Kate to accompany her to the ladies room, though Mr. Fairweather who just quaintly smiled suspected we were on to them.

I knew this fox and his buddy "popeye" just didn't want us at the head table to talk about shrimp and aged wine but rather was on a fact-finding mission to sell a story for his magazine if he could get it.

While initially discussing mundane facts Nikki returned from the ladies room without Kate leaving me to wonder if she was just given a heads up to what I was going to do.

Mr. Fairweather then revealed his opening hand, by asking, "Frank, there's talk in certain circles that there is a problem in space and that the governments of the earth are very concerned. Is there any truth to that?"

I replied, "Not that I am aware of Mr. Fairweather. Hmm….news to me."

Mr. Fairweather stated, "Perhaps I was too direct, Frank. Let me put it another way, in the "People's War," are we winning?"

Nikki looked at me as I was struggling for an answer that said everything yet meant nothing and interjected, "Jim, Frank here is just a fighter pilot and he does not have access to such information if it existed."

Mr. Fairweather looked at Nikki and stated, "Okay sweetheart, you'll do. Is there a war in space? Are we winning the "People's War?"

Nikki shot back, "Jim, I have been known to stretch the truth at times which comes with my position, but I can't bring myself to lying. So my answer to you is no and don't know!"

Mr. Fairweather quickly asked, "Well, who would know Nikki?"

Nikki replied, "With all due respect, Mr. Fairweather, the Pentagon might, but I am not sure."

Mr. Fairweather asked, "Nikki I thought you were in intelligence?"

"I am," stated Nikki, "But only at the squadron level, Mr. Fairweather. Hope that helps?"

Mr. Fairweather chuckled, "How's the wine, Frank? Would you like another glass?"

"Sure," I said laughing, "You buying?"

Mr. Fairweather chuckled some more and stated, "Sure, what are good friends for?"

My ass, I thought, yet stated, "Yes, nothing like being in the company of good friends."

Suddenly Mr. Fairweather's pal "Popeye" jumped in the fray and started staring at my medals on my chest with curiosity through what looked like his glass eye and asked what they meant and stood for.

I explained to "Popeye" certain medals like my distinguished flying cross and my two Medal of Honors.

Jack then queried, "I was unaware you won the Medal of Honor twice, Frank?"

I replied, "Jack some campaign medals are awarded in secret."

This reply left Mr. Fairweather and Jack, high and dry, thinking indeed I was awarded for an engagement in a secret war unbeknown to them.

Mr. Fairweather apparently did not like the tone of my voice, so I stated to Nikki and Mr. Fairweather as I watched Kate walk by if they would excuse me for a moment.

As I walked up to Kate, she appeared sheepish when she saw me approaching at the hors d'oeuvres table.

"Hello Kate, how are you doing tonight?" I asked, "I wanted to talk to you at the Oscars but the event did not offer an opportunity.

It's been a long time Kate; I felt I was worthy of a warm hello or a nod to say the least. I feel I'm worth that."

Kate replied, "I'm fine Frank and you?"

As I looked at Kate I could see the sadness in her eyes, "I'm fine Kate. How's your acting career going. I could see on the Oscars itinerary that you were not mentioned for any possible awards."

"Haven't you heard Frank?" as Kate looked at me inquisitively.

Playing dumb, I stated, "Heard what?"

"That I am divorced with two small children," Kate angrily stated.

I responded, "No, I didn't know Kate. I am sorry to hear that. May I ask what happened?"

Kate looked at me with such bitterness, "Mike was a cross-dresser, he liked women and men. Especially men and my Southern Baptist religion doesn't accept that and nor did I. So he had to go, it was that simple, Frank."

"I'm sorry to hear that Kate. What are your plans now?" I asked.

Kate replied, "There are no plans. My acting career was destroyed by Mike's antics and I am left in the middle of nowhere between somewhere and elsewhere.

I'm the laughing stock of Hollywood and Broadway and I'll be out in the streets in no time waiting on tables in some short order cook restaurant.

I should have listened to you, Frank, but the glitter of Hollywood and the lights of Broadway blinded me to the truth.

I can't recover from this alone Frank.

Sorry to cry on your shoulder."

I looked at Kate as she gazed into my eyes and that old feeling came back to me about her, as a matter-of-fact it never left, "Kate, you still have my option opened to you. I never stopped caring for you from the moment I seen you in Central Park.

Come with me Kate?"

Kate looked at me with admiration and softly stated, "You are still a good man, Frank, and in my eyes will always be, but now I have children from another man and I cannot burden you with that."

"Kate," as I held her arm, "I'll love your children like my own and where we're going we can start anew and there will be no shame *placed before my queen!"*

As Kate put her arms around me, I embraced her with the deepest most tenderness kiss I could give a woman. Kate cried deeply from the heart as she laid her head against my chest while I held her in my arms.

"So you will come now, Kate?" I asked her.

Kate replied while weeping heavily, "Frank, I hoped for this but I never thought you would ever take me back again."

I asked again, "So you will come with me Kate, with your children?"

Kate looked at me with relief and stated, "I will Frank!"

"Good," I said, "Kate get your house in order and be prepared to leave at a moment's notice. Take just the clothes on your back and keep a luggage case by the side of your bed, nothing more."

Kate looked at me with concern and stated, "Is it that bad Frank …are we still losing?"

As I looked at Kate with concern, I stated, "It's worse then breaking bad Kate for we have two invasion fleets approaching earth and yes, we have lost every main battle against the Gigantopithecus up till today, and tomorrow will be no different.

So stay ready, at all times, Kate, for I will come swiftly for you like a thief in the night."

Kate replied, "I'll be ready Frank. I'll wait for you."

I looked at Kate, and stated in no uncertain terms, "Kate wait for me, however long it takes wherever you are, wait for me.

For I will come quickly and find you and take you with me so where I am you shall be also.

Now I must go Kate."

As I returned back to the table where Nikki and Mr. Fairweather were chatting, I informed Mr. Fairweather that Nikki and I had to get back to the squadron to check on flight operations and thanked him for his fine hospitality.

Chapter 12-The Revelation

In the upcoming days while the intelligent agencies of the earth were trying to determine the depth of the Giganthepitecus penetration among the inhabitants of the earth, I decided with council to activate the dead man's switch to prepare for destruction of the earth and it's inhabitants.

We decided to transmit on all open frequencies that the Giants and the Giganthopithecus were known to use for communication that numerous individuals of earths 7 billion population were wired in a "Dead Man's switch" to destroy the earth if an all out invasion occurred.

The governments of the earth and the High Council unanimously agreed that the earth would not become a slave colony to the invading host.

But could I do it? My hands trembled at the thought of it.

I was further instructed by the High Council to make known earths situation to its inhabitants so that they could get their house in order and prepare to meet their God.

It was determined that in the following days I would make my speech on the Bettermen's Show before a live television audience.

It would be there where I would declare the dilemma facing the inhabitants of earth and further inform them of my position regarding this matter.

When the date came for the Bettermen Show, I entered again with all the fanfare as before. Upon sitting down and apparently for Neilson rating reasons Kate walks on stage to greet me.

Needless to say I was delighted, yet, surprised.

Bettermen was slightly guarded not knowing precisely what may transpire before him. Yet, as I thought about it, the fanfare it would draw would be an even bigger audience than I could have hoped for without Kate.

As we got midway into the show, the question from Bettermen kept coming up on what is going on in the South China Sea, the "People's War" and really whom am I?

Bettermen apparently setting a trap for me, per the powers that be on his television network, asked directly, "Frank, there has been numerous letters from our audience wanting to know the answer to some questions. Can you cut to the quick, cut through the bull and tell our audience what in the hell is really going on in this so called "People's War?"

Lastly, who are you really Frank?"

As I stood up and took the floor, I said, "It's time, Mr. Bettermen for you and the human race to know the complete truth."

I nodded to Omega and Tron to come on stage and told them, "Tell the powers that be on this broadcasting network that there will be no commercial breaks until I am finished talking.

Enforce it if need be!"

Omega and Tron nodded their head in the affirmative and placed their right hand on their heart signaling that they will fulfill my command.

The audience became uneasy to my authoritative command and change of personality. They became silent and curious as to what was transpiring in front of them for they realized that for whatever reason, I had the power and authority and not their government to do and say what must be said and done.

Bettermen was taken aback for I have just overrode any power or leverage he thought he had in regards to his say for the broadcasting station and the reason would be explained now within moments on his show.

Immediately, as I addressed the audience I went into an extended reply that all I have said in the past was a deliberate lie.

I then told the audience a shocking revelation that, *"I am a son of god, but **not** the Son of God, Jesus Christ, the Eternal One."*

I told them that, "I am a descendant of a race known as the Anunnaki from the planet Nibiru, the tenth planet in this solar system that orbits beyond the planet Pluto.

We look just like humans as you can see, I look like an ordinary human being...but I am not human...............I am an Anunnaki.

The Anunnaki people reside here on earth in the area of Baalbek, Lebanon near Ankoun and Masgara for these are the people of the book.

We have walked among you since time everlasting because you humans are our creation. We walked the earth before your creation for we have existed long before your race was created.

You humans are a hybrid race, a genetic mixture from an original indigenous being of the earth created by the Son of God, known as the Giganthopithecus and from us, the race of the Anunnaki's, who reside on Nibiru, the tenth planet in this solar system.

This hominid being known as the Gigantopithecus is a gigantic bi-pedal, a carnivore and herbivore that roamed the earth for hundreds of thousands of years.

I then told them that, "I am an anointed prince that soon will become king of my planet Nibiru and governor of this planet who will rule with justice and mercy and not in the fashion that the slithering powers that be do here today.

But until that day I have been dispatched to procreate with selected females of *"the daughters of men"* to advance mankind both intellectually and spiritually."

The audience was silent, you could hear a pin drop.

I then said, "This elegant lady sitting next to me, Kate Winely, is to be a queen of a new hybrid human race selected for her advanced genetic makeup of Anunnaki and human genes."

Kate looked at me with a concerned curious look.

Bettermen was frozen in time and space methodically analyzing every word I mentioned.

As I continued, "This new hybrid race we are about to create will not be a servant to us as before which was designed to gather gold to sustain our atmosphere and to increase our longevity. But rather this new race will become a partner with us, a symbiotic relationship if you like, to advance both our species."

As I looked around at the spellbound crowd, I asked, "Are there any questions?"

There were none.

As I looked at Bettermen, I stated, "You wanted to know Mr. Bettermen what was going on in space and who I was? Did I answer your question?"

Mr. Bettermen nodded his head.

I asked, "Mr. Bettermen, do you have any further questions?"

He stated solemnly, "No, Frank….I was expecting some sort of show biz answer; instead I got "War of the Worlds."

As I looked away from Mr. Bettermen, I quickly faced the audience to state, "As the saying goes Mr. Bettermen, be careful what you wish for, for it may come true. That said I will continue.

In the days that we created you, approximately 350,000 years ago as a "hybrid being" derived from part Anunnaki and part Gigantopithecus, we all lived in harmony upon the earth.

But conflict followed and certain members of our race fought for control of the earth against the wishes of others.

The humans we created were forced to become involved in our conflict so we taught them warfare along with the Gigantopithecus.

Under the direction of Amen-Ra, a warlike Anunnaki who is my great uncle whom the people of Egypt had worshipped as, *Ra,* the races ended up fighting against each other.

During this warfare and ongoing conflict many Anunnaki's decided to leave earth and return to their home planet due to perpetual chaos, much like humans flee the ghettos from humans who are hardwired for violence. During this time animosity grew between the races especially between the humans and Gigantopithecus.

The Gigantopithecus believed that they were the original beings created by God of the Universe to inhabit the earth and that we, the Anunnaki, were invaders and opportunists who created this hybrid mutated race, the humans, against the divine order. The humans in turn eventually took over the planet against the will of the Gigantopithecus and destroyed their way of life, much like what the white man did to the Indians in these United States.

During the days of the flood of Noah, approximately 13,500 years ago around 11,500 B.C. a deluge occurred upon the whole earth. It was a natural occurrence and had nothing to do with the gods or the Anunnaki. It was the will of the Creator of All to stop and end the carnage.

The Anunnaki fled the earth to Mars with certain selected earth women *who were* **fair** *and beautiful of which they took as wives as many as they chose.*

During this time on earth food was scarce and so the Gigantopithecus demanded that the humans along with serving the remaining Anunnaki also bring them food to eat. When the humans faltered, due to a diminishing food supply, the Gigantopithecus began eating the smaller humans by demanding human sacrifices at the temple of the Mayans and Aztecs.

Moreover, the giant Gigantopithecus began raping the human women and splitting them in two during sexual intercourse.

It was at this time an angelic emissary from God of the Universe was dispatched to destroy almost all the Gigantopithecus on the earth leaving the remnant of them to flee into space into the caves of Mars.

It was in these caves that the Anunnaki in olden times hid their most destructive planetary weapons. The Gigantopithecus inadvertently discovered these weapons of mass destruction unbeknown to us and studied them in great detail.

During the thousands of years that passed since the flood, the Gigantopithecus studied these weapons to the degree that they could now reverse engineer them until they could master the weapons.

When we, the Anunnaki, returned as we do every few thousand years to the Mars Way Station, we were met with an unwelcome committee on Mars.

We found to our dismay millions of Gigantopithecus waiting for us in the caves and underground of Mars. Horrific battles ensued and it was during this time we learned the merciless ways of the Gigantopithecus. They would always fight to the death, never surrender, kill all their prisoners and refuse to negotiate. It was total war in it's purest form, scorched earth, total annihilation of a species.... winner take all.

Kate asked in a concerned and hurtful manner, as she began to cry out loud, "Does that mean Frank our relationship was an absolute lie and cover story?"

I then stated to her, "My love for you, Kate, was and is true for because of you I am here. For the girl inside you must leave, for the woman within you is screaming to come out since time eternal, for she is a queen bee of a new race.

It is you, Kate, that I have come for so as to be my spouse forever and to start a new race. You along with six other women queen's genes are compiled together for genetic variance to create a race. I could not force sex on you then because you have chosen another. For when I started seeing you, Kate, the girl inside you chose Mike Mountain in error.

Yet, the queen strain inside of you rejected him as an eternal mate. So I had to wait until time began running out to determine if you would finally choose me freely or force me perhaps to steal you which violated all rules and regulations of the High Council.

If you did not chose me or if I didn't steal you, this new human species would not be created and you along with many other humans would die in this upcoming tribulation and divinely designed cataclysm.

The tribulation will begin by the presence of a "dark being" that is yet to be identified who will rule from the Temple Mount in Jerusalem.

While the cataclysm will begin with a warning, then followed by a divine miracle and finished with three days of darkness, that is the final chastisement from our Eternal Creator for lack of sincere repentance upon your race.

For have you not read this in your bible when Moses put up his hands and the world underwent three days of darkness.

A cloaked object, a ship, will cause the three days of darkness. This ship will be 77,000 miles across in diameter, which will cross between the orbit of the earth and Venus. It will be from this ship, that divine angels will come forth to bind and burn these unselected wicked humans who are controlled by demons from the dark side.

Just as it happened during the days of Noah and during the Jewish exodus, it will happen again.

Yet, this event will be unpredictable for this "destroyer" ship will cloak itself as a comet yet be under intelligent control.

So you see Kate, it was then when you divorced this boy man that the woman inside you took over your being and demanded a more genetically evolved male. I couldn't kill Mike Mountain, this boy man, for this is a similar problem that we, Anunnaki had with the "Dykes" on my planet, Nibiru, which nearly destroyed my world.

You now have chose me and stated you loved me on three different occasions, which by the council's rules of engagement from the Great Hall of my people, I qualify to be your spouse and you mine."

I then stated to Bettermen, "You and the audience have a small window of time left to ask me all the questions you feel is relevant to your survival for those of you who may be *left behind* and I will attempt to answer them to the best of my ability. Your time of questioning starts now then I must go and return to the front.

Remember, I am talking about the extermination of a species, them or us...total annihilation."

Bettermen then asked, "My God, what you just said Frank is so ominous, if what we earthlings are seeing are not planes in the skies then what are they....UFO's?"

I stated, "Yes, Mr. Bettermen...they are UFO'S...and their not ours!

Moreover, the claim that I shot down numerous Mig fighters in aerial combat over the South China Sea was a lie, for the truth of the matter is what I shot down was enemy hostiles known to us as UFO's.

They were shot down in deep space between the earth and moon. They are an invading force that we first met in the caves of Mars.

The Gigantopithecus entered the Cydonia Complex on Mars and stole the ancient artifacts from a dead king of ours, King Alalu who was buried there over 350,000 years ago. With all respect for our king who discovered that gold existed in abundant quantities on earth we left in his tomb our advanced ancient technology untouched.

The gold on earth we entrusted humans to collect was to be harvested for our planet, Nibiru, whose dwindling atmosphere was creating catastrophic weather conditions. Our scientists finally realized that the gold element in dust form would stabilize our atmosphere and return weather conditions back to normal.

Moreover, gold was used as a staple in our diet, which further contributed to long life of our species by reversing the aging processes. This in turn allowed us to live between 500,000 years to one million years each by your earth years. So as you can see, gold was critical to our survival as a species.

We created humans who were a hybrid between Gigantopithecus and us. The human mission was simple, which was "to gather gold in abundant amount" to be processed and shipped back to Nibiru.

However, during the days of Noah, the Gigantopithecus were nearly exterminated to the last one by the Creator of All for raping and murdering "The Daughters of Men."

129

They, the Giganthopitecus fled to Mars where they were allowed to live out their days unhindered until the end of this age.

Yet, little did we know that the Gigantopithecus had a significant mental capacity to learn complex things?

While we were away for a significant amount of time from our Mars outpost, the Mars Way Station, the Gigantopithecus discovered the Cydonia Complex of our deceased king. The Gigantopithecus then stole the ancient artifacts of which many were advanced weapons of war that we created and kept off our planet Nibiru in order to maintain peace.

The Gigantopithecus in their zeal to learn realized that our ancient artifacts left behind at Cydonia were weapons of mass destruction. Upon realizing that they had these advance weapons in their hands they quickly learned how to adapt them to their advantage.

Against this backdrop, the Gigantopithecus decided to go on the offensive to take their home planet, the Earth back. Upon finding this out, our intelligence units in the field interrogated captured high ranking Gigantopithecus on Mars and discovered that their true intentions was not just conquest of Earth but the solar system as a whole including Nibiru.

Needless to say, we were shocked when we discovered on Mars how the Gigantopithecus had technologically advanced their race so significant that they caused enormous losses to our personnel and equipment from battles on Mars.

The ensuing battles had such a high degree of mortality rate and casualties that we could not sustain the losses that the Gigantopithecus could, especially with their lack of concern for their own life.

We then decided to enter into an agreement with leaders of the human race that if they made an alliance with us we would no longer treat the humans as a slave race but as partners.

We needed enormous amounts of human soldiers and the leaders of the earth in return wanted advanced technology to improve the earth's human population's living conditions.

Seeing that the earth is already heavily overpopulated and the governments of the earth had millions of soldiers to spare both sides agreed quickly to each other's demand and signed an alliance for our preservation.

We further negotiated with your leaders that whatever the human armies discovered advanced technology from the Gigantopithecus this technology or "booty" was theirs to keep. From this alliance that was drafted between our races is the very reason why since Roswell your race has advanced exponentially technologically over the last few decades.

Furthermore, as far as human abduction is concerned, there were only those select females with high Anunnaki genes that we experimented with in order to find out which of your race were carriers of our strain. The women were placed back in their beds unhurt and not sexually molested.

As far as cattle mutilations that were witnessed all over the globe, this was the handy work of the Gigantopithecus who had a taste for meat since there were no cows on Mars and to further cloak their children as humans by extracting genetic material.

Despite all this, when we completed our reconnaissance on Mars we found that the Gigantopithecus had evolved so much militarily that they formed a formidable army placing both our species in grave danger of extinction. Since the war began, we have lost every major battle against the Gigantopithecus, so much so, that our combined fleets are on the run from Mars and elsewhere and are now fleeing towards earth as I speak."

Bettermen shocked asked, "From Mars?"

I said, "Yes."

Bettermen then attempting to confirm what he just heard asked, "Are you saying that we are on Mars?"

"I am saying, Mr. Bettermen, that my race has been on Mars for hundred of thousands of years in the past and your race joined us briefly in the Cydonia Complex Wars until we were ambushed and overrun by a superior enemy force.

Initially, there were one thousand of Anunnaki's and humans from the planet Nibiru and Earth returning to reactivate an advance Way Station on Mars and to await the main force from Nibiru for our return to earth.

It was later affirmed via intelligence that our main force could possibly destroy the Gigantopithecus outright, but the risk and casualties would be high. For we knew from the beginning conflicts that the Gigantopithecus in the caves on Mars were ruthless for they annihilated our prisoners without mercy and refused outright to any negotiations.

So as things now stand, we await our fleeing fleets from Mars and it's moons, the out planets with the hopes that our main Anunnaki invasion fleet still enroute from the far reaches of our solar system can turn the tide of the war.

Moreover, I am not a Captain but a General of a once elite commando division, which was the best of the Anunnaki and human military that could be assembled.

Now, all that is left from this thousand-man elite force is Lt. Hill, Lt. Calloway, myself and three others who are hospitalized in critical condition. Which means of the 1,000 men and women I started with there are only six of us left which should tell you how vicious the Giganthopithecus really are.

With this in mind, I have to make you aware that there is no army of ours presently in place right now above Earth to fight the Gigantopithecus except for our retreating space fleet that is returning back to the Earth to a defensive position.

So you see, ladies and gentlemen, despite what the Gigantopithecus claim of the Earth, in the beginning of time the gods fought for space and we acquired the Earth and the solar system as our booty."

Bettermen then asked, "What do they the Gigantopithecus look like?"

I stated, "They are gigantic in size relative to us, Anunnaki and humans. They are about eight to ten feet tall and resemble hairy giant apes that stand erect. Their strength is incredible for they can kill instantly any polar or grizzly bear in hand-to-hand combat.

That said and to make matters worse yet, there is another fleet from an unknown race, a massive armada approaching us as well.

Intentions unknown!

This armada of Giants which are known by the Vatican and other intelligence agencies throughout the world to be approaching us have forced these agencies to prepare a speech of "first contact" to present to the people of the Earth.

These unknown races of Giants were first spotted in the rings of Saturn with starships in excess of 75,000 miles long and up to 300,000 miles long. When one considers the Earth's diameter is a little less then 8,000 miles then one can readily see how frightening and overwhelming this problem is that we are facing.

Again, the life forms that exist within these crafts are 26 miles tall, which is further beyond all our comprehension.

This is incomprehensible to us, yet it is true. Our long-range sensors on Mars's, moon Phobos, picked up these capital ships inbound.

We further discovered the Giants on Earth's moon in the southern quadrant near the Zeeman crater that has led us to believe that your moon is an ancient ship of theirs and they are in the process of activating it for whatever reason.

This is why your United States satellite LCROSS and the Indian satellite Chandrayaan who were studying the southern quadrant of the moon were destroyed or captured in 2009.

Their Giants smallest ship, a scout ship, as far as we can tell is 178 miles long and contains one 26 mile tall "being."

We do not know what star system they came from that would allow such an enormous size creature to evolve nor do we know what exactly is their precise intention. Yet, they made it clear to us in no uncertain terms to stay off the moon and stay away from them.

As far as we know these Giants are a class three civilization, which draw energy from all the stars in a galaxy, while a class two-civilization draws energy from a solar system's star. A class one civilization, like us, the Anunnaki, draws energy from the planet's sun itself, while the humans of the Earth are a class zero civilization, which rely on fossil fuels for energy."

A man from the audience yelled out, "C,mon, beings 26 miles tall?"

I replied, "Yes, you've heard that correct, beings 26 miles tall! Their intentions are unknown but they appear to be robots mining on the moons in our galaxy, we cannot defeat them due to their immense size.

Moreover, they appear to have as many ships and personnel as we have. We first thought they were angels from the Eternal One, but we are unsure now for we have never encountered beings of this massive size."

Kate, was crying and shaking with fear for the welfare of her family asked, "Then we are losing, Frank?"

I looked at her angelic crying eyes and stated softly as I held her soft hands, "Yes Kate we are losing and that's why I have come back for you. For you are a queen, like your ancestor Eve was and you along with six other selected queens must be rescued to a safe location to ensure the procreation of both our species.

I have to get you out of here Kate before some genetically inferior and irresponsible man who is not a man ruins you."

As I turned back towards the audience I stated, "I want to explain to you who we, "the sons of god" are to you? For as it is stated in Genesis in your Holy Bible that the "sons of god", looked down upon the Earth and realized that "the daughters of men" were **fair** and beautiful and my ancestors took them as *wives* "as many as they chose."

Now seven of us "sons of god" were selected to mate with your women to improve and upgrade your genetic stock, but unbeknown to me, Kate, I found out that you were a queen.

That is, Kate, your genetic makeup has an extremely high degree of Anunnaki genes and for that reason alone the procreation process between us will create an genetic stock almost as superior as the Anunnaki race.

Due to your highly evolved advanced genetic makeup nearly equaling a Anunnaki queen on my planet the Supreme Council from the Great Hall of my people decreed through secret communiqué not to tell me at the time when I first met you that my mission was considered a suicide mission, for it was believed you would detect me and with your pheromones destroy me immediately.

Moreover, as a colony queen, in waiting, you could not be taken by force, which is the death penalty for me without exception. For that is the ancient way of murdering your spouse's mate to accomplish your mission. In the past that type of thinking led to the near destruction of our home world, Nibiru, but since then the law of selection now clearly states, your spouse to be must be allowed to chose you freely and openly without restrictions or hindrance.

When you told me, you were engaged to be married it came as another surprise to me. Yet, when I first met you I realized I arrived too late in your life. For you had given up as most women on Earth regrettably do, waiting for that knight in shining armor to come, so in desperation you married.

Despite the law of selection and choice of mate I honored to the end, it almost compelled me for the sake of our races to violate the sacred decrees from the High Council. Our only hope then was the random probability and possibility of a divorce from that boy man you chose in desperation to marry.

You realize, Kate that you were infatuated with him and that he, a failure both morally and ethically, further could not fulfill your natural desires despite his best effort.

So when your divorce took place, as I believed it would, you realized the error of your ways and returned to me, for only an Anunnaki male can fulfill the natural desires of a colony queen.

So it was then I had to intervene and take you as my love spouse for eternity.

That said, to you the audience and people of the Earth, as to the war in space, our Anunnaki numbers are few and your human numbers are large yet our technology was vastly superior to yours.

We could not win alone against the Gigantopithecus due to our lack in numbers; yet, with you as our allies we had a fighting chance.

So we formed an alliance with the governments of the Earth where our means of producing aircraft in large quantities in conjunction with the plentiful of your human resource base allowed us to field a large military force.

Yet, despite all this we are still losing an incredible amount of human and Anunnaki personnel."

"How many?" Bettermen asked

I stated, "To understand the depth of the carnage, Mr. Bettermen, last month alone, the Chinese who are our allies, along with Russia and the United States have lost a considerable amount of personnel.

The Chinese lost 15,000 pilots just last month alone, while the Russians lost nearly 10,000 and the United States lost 3,000 pilots from their deep space program.

The classified raids you heard about in the South China Sea was a diversion from the truth, the real raids took place on Mars and the Moon where some of our pilots were captured who had privy to our most guarded battle secrets and had to be rescued before they would be tortured to confess.

That's why Kate when you seen my hands burnt it came from an explosive charge from a sapper Giganthopithecus and from charges that I had set to free our captured men.

This in turn led to Lt. Calloway, Lt. Hill and myself, all aces, to be awarded the Congressional Medal of Honor. For the record officially, though the true unofficial record is much higher, Lt. Calloway has ten aircraft kills, Lt. Hill has five aircraft kills as for myself, I have sixteen enemy aircraft destroyed.

Furthermore, those two men I just mentioned are carriers of high percentage Anunnaki genes like me and those two wonderful women you see them with who are to be their wives are also high carriers of advanced Anunnaki genes.

As far as Capt. Nikki Aliz, she was also selected to be taken as a concubine if I failed with you, Kate, for Nikki also has a high percentage of Anunnaki genetics and despite her reluctance to get married for the love of her mother, protocol of a species preservation and creation supersedes her mother's care.

So as you can see Kate, both you and Nikki have an exceptional amount of Anunnaki blood and both of you I deeply love, yet, you are preferred for you are a queen with primary Anunnaki genes born to procreate a new race alone if need be.

Nikki due to her love to be a nun left the Church to tend to her sickly mother and wouldn't marry. While you married a boy-man, a ladder climber, who didn't care about you from the beginning but just your money and to further use you to elevate his career. My concern came when I realized your awareness of your situation when you refused to deal with the realization that Mike Mountain played you so you attempted to buy his love with more of your money, which in turn failed miserably.

Finally, within your heart, the girl inside you had to step aside for the real woman who violently abhorred and rejected being bedded by a parasite.

Obviously, at that time for the future is unwritten, it appeared I was going to lose both you, Kate and Nikki. Yet, I had to wait until the last moment in time with this cataclysmic upheaval about to occur coupled with a multipronged invasion at our doorstep. In essence, time was running out against us all and the procreation of an advance human species would have been in dire jeopardy.

Regarding the matter of the Gigantopithecus, there has been an advance guard of them walking among you for thousands of your years.

The Gigantopithecus believe not only the Creator of All killed them at the time of the deluge but also they believe we, the Anunnaki, murdered them also at this time without just cause.

So their hatred for us, the Anunnaki, runs deep with them.

You also asked me Kate if I ever killed and I stated sixteen, which is correct but they were not humans but Gigantopithecus who cloaked themselves in human form in which we cannot detect until their nearly on top of us.

We are hoping with our home fleet approaching with new energy beam weapons that we can turn the tide, but the best way for you and the audience to know if we are holding the line is that you are alive.

It is the simplest and best indicator."

"My god," Bettermen stated "Are you serious, this has to be a bad dream? C'mon this can't be real."

I came back and stated, "Mr. Bettermen, in what you just seen and heard especially taking control of all the television networks, do you really think I would sit here before these just and fair American people and lie?"

Bettermen came back, "I guess not."

I then replied, "Mr. Bettermen, in the last battle alone I lost fifteen pilots from a squadron of twenty-one.

Furthermore, how many of America's satellites went missing on Mars or lost communication for no apparent reason. Plus, why would your nation send military Clemintine satellites to the moon to survey the moon when you have no intention of returning there?

Why do you think you have not returned to the moon since 1969 when shear probability since that time states that you should be out to the planet Pluto?

Why would certain female French astronauts with advance degrees in genetics and biology be overheard screaming as they were being dragged away while declaring during a nervous breakdown, **"The people of the earth must be warned?"**

Why has the Vatican now declared that the probability of life elsewhere could exist and that God is universal?

Why has the Vatican built a telescope on Mt. Graham Arizona on a sacred Indian burial ground and named their telescope, "Lucifer", which is more powerful then Hubble?

The people of the Earth apparently are under the watchful eyes of the controlling parties on Earth who would not want to make you aware of this ongoing confrontation with the Gigantopithecus and the Giants, for they do not want you to know what's approaching the Earth or it's ominous intentions.

That's why!

The UFO's you earth people have been seeing in your sky's for about 50 years now are the advance guard from the Gigantopithecus who are using organic gray alien robots for abductions.

Our forces are losing yet holding back this advance guard for the moment, but their main invasion force we cannot hold without assistance from my planet.

Unless our main battles fleet and our sister planets armada arrive on time we will lose.

The Earth, in this time frame, is now as it was in the days of Noah which has become unacceptable to the Eternal Creator for All for He has instructed His angelic force to destroy the entire planet except for a remnant that He is taking in an event called the Rapture and the remnant that we are taking for procreation of a new species.

My race, the Anunnaki from the planet Nibiru and our earthly remnants on earth here whose last names are **Anon, Anoun, Aon, Anun, and further derivatives from the word Anunnaki** reside near the landing area of Baalbek, Lebanon who created humans as a hybrid race from the Anunnaki and Gigantopithecus to do manual labor for us.

In return for your slave work we accelerated your evolutionary development millions of years in a relatively short period of time. Through our constant perfection and manipulation of the human species we continually injected our advance genetic makeup, with your genes, to make you to take on more and more responsibility and complex roles. Because of our continual upgrading of your human species you became almost identical to looking as us. However, our longevity was denied humans until you could evolve

138

socially, mentally and spiritually, which could only be acquired through constant rebirth, experience and time.

Furthermore, humans could only acquire our vast superior intelligence, which we gained through long life over an extended period of time. But since we each lived beyond 500,000 of your Earth years, your human life span at best was pitiful compared to ours.

The best a human's life span length could obtain was when it approached nearly 1,000 years before the flood and this dropped dismally to about 120 years after the flood.

But as luck would have it, it was discovered that Anunnaki children raised on Earth developed five times faster then on Nibiru. However, it was further discovered that despite the excellent growth acceleration that the Anunnaki children developed on Earth had as compared to their Nibiru counterparts, Earth children were growing at a still much higher acceleration rate and therefore were evolving faster then the Anunnaki children were per unit of time.

It was then realized in the Great Hall of my people before the Supreme Council that if the human species were left unchecked they would accelerate past the Anunnaki in intelligence and ultimately use us as their slaves.

In order to prevent this we therefore had to create diverse pagan religions in order to impede your intelligence growth and spiritual development. We further stopped infusing Anunnaki genes into your race so as to hinder your genetic admixture, which further retarded your mental growth.

We then allowed human proxies to be used as our brokers to rule men of whom you call "Royalty", "the Illuminati", or "The Powers That Be."

These proxies created wars in order to maintain their power base and slowed your growth development even further.

As horrible as that sounds to you humans regarding our affairs over men, consider how far you have evolved technologically in the last hundred years. Yet, without proper control mechanisms in place your race would be like the Gigantopithecus, a savage, warlike and cruel race.

Regrettably, your race began to become recessive due to the extermination of your healthy intelligent males through war attrition while the unfit was allowed to breed.

It was then discovered that without the constant influx of Anunnaki genes humankind through constant copulation among themselves were creating diluted and genetically inferior beings who were paganistic and hardwired for crime.

Your inner cities are a testimonial to this where drugs, violence, family breakdowns with sub-human intelligence abound.

That is, your race was digressing back to the Gigantopithecus hominid from which you came. As your race regressed further you were becoming irresponsible, senseless and therefore undesirable for complex tasks as directed by our Supreme Council.

However, the human woman was not genetically recessing as quickly as her male counterpart so it was decided that certain select women on Earth, that were carrying a majority of Anunnaki traits, would be saved for procreation elsewhere after the cataclysm which is soon to come from space.

In this way, we the Anunnaki made your race even more sophisticated, more advance and more technologically intelligent at an accelerated rate.

So much so, that my male ancestors, found, the women of Earth to be much more desirable then our own females who had lost their own feminine charm and became hardened and cold with an insatiable lust for power and wealth.

But the earth women were different, for they were young in spirit and warm in heart and loving to behold. They were **fair** and caring and irresistible to my male ancestors who took them for wives as much as they chose.

Our male Anunnaki could not resist the Earth women and this caused a great upheaval at the Supreme Council in the Great Hall of my people. The council realized that we were downgrading our own species by marrying "the daughters of men."

While our own females were left unmarried, abandoned, not chosen and brokenhearted.

So the Great Council therefore punished my forefathers for breeding with "the daughters of men" and condemned them for falling in love with *the daughters of m*en."

So they were cast out of heaven as believed fallen angels to the Earth, but heaven in this context was Nibiru and the fallen angels were Anunnaki.

Yet, despite that, my forefathers accepted their fate and continued to marry earth women, despite the edicts forbidding so from the High Council. In essence then, we became like the sailors in the novel, <u>Mutiny on the Bounty</u>, where my ancestors married the natives and refused to return home.

For my male ancestors would rather have a short romantic love affair with *"the daughters of men"* then be miserable with our combative feminist Anunnaki females.

The Earth women desired my forefathers for their intelligence and kindness so they bore them children, men of renown.

My forefathers were then told again to change their ways per a decree from the council, but the Anunnaki males still refused the edict and continued choosing earth women, which placed our race in disarray.

That said, so now for the first time, the people of the Earth have heard the true story from "the sons of god" regarding matters of your existence, why you are here, where your going and what's it all about.

It wasn't that we, the Anunnaki were evil, it wasn't that we were bad, it was just that our love for *"the daughters of men"* we couldn't resist. Your women who we chose to accompany us throughout our existence relieved us from our loneliness and brought happiness and sunshine into our lives.

Nobody knew at the time that our genetic manipulation of humans would create irresistible women on the Earth…how could anyone have predicted this?

What followed then was the council condemned us to leave our planet, Nibiru, to Mars, the earth's oceans or deep within the earth. That's where we have been ever since, but this planet is dying and per the council, of which we still have our allegiance too we must evacuate selected women from the Earth.

To complicate and make matters worse the Eternal One sent an ambassador informing us through omens and dreams that we were to be punished for mating with lower order life forms since the flood.

Our fate was sealed, until the time of our punishment was over which is the end of this age, yet our love for *"the daughters of men"* has never wavered, not one bit.

As for my love for you, Kate, I find you irresistible, vulnerable and warm. You are life itself and without you I have no existence and I dream alone.

When I met you Kate, despite your antics and shortsightedness I realized for the first time why my ancestors couldn't resist *"the daughters of men"* and would rather die with you then without you.

Kate now crying stated, "Frank, though I love you, I can't go, I have children."

"Kate," I stated, "I will love your children as if they were my own, for anything that is yours I would love them forever."

Kate still crying embraced me and kissed me with a deep passionate kiss.

As I looked back at the audience, I stated, "As far as Tron and Omega, they are my guardians, given to my race from the ancient ones who created our race.

As far as you the audience, the signs of the times are here and have been overwhelmingly neglected despite the obvious times. Yet intuitively, you sensed this by the changes occurring on the earth and smelled it in the air, that is, the uneasiness of something unknown and ominous approaching you.

What were you thinking in these two thousand years, that the Son of Man from the Eternal One was an act in futility?

The proof of your shortsightedness is having children today which is tantamount to placing a young tomato plant in a northern hemisphere garden in November to grow, knowing that it will not reach fruition.

For how is it, that you understand the signs of the weather but not the signs of the times?"

The audience looked in disbelief, brokenhearted and stunned as if they were just handed a death penalty.

As I concluded, "Your only hope is that you have been found to be of the selected seed that will be chosen by the Son of Man in an event you call the Rapture, if not you will be left behind to settle your accounts with your creator in an event known as the tribulation."

When their time was up, Kate and I walked off the stage leaving Bettermen and the audience in total silence.

Chapter 13-The Scene

The following day, Kate and I attended the Directors Guild of America in West Hollywood in Oceania Park adjacent to the Pacific Ocean. As Kate, Nikki and Oceania were seated at the front table, I looked at Tron and Omega to affirm if everything was in order.

With their slight bow and right hand across their heart they confirmed and saluted me the decree by the Supreme Council from the Great Hall of my people that I must inform and prepare the people of the Earth today of an approaching invasion fleet from space.

As I walked up on the stage to the podium on this bright and sunny windswept day watching the glistening waves of the Pacific Ocean ebbing to and fro mesmerized me. As I crossed the stage I was captivated by the beauty of the moment as I observed surfers riding the waves in simple enjoyment of life without care or concern.

As I scanned the crowd my eyes were magnetically drawn to the shapely female beauties that lightly moved across my bow like palm trees gently blowing in the wind. They walked before me adorned in their eloquent garb as if Athena goddesses from the temple Parthenon on the Acropolis in Greece, in days long gone by.

This moment compelled me to wonder if this was how it was when my great ancestors addressed Noah and his people during the upcoming days of the deluge.

As I stepped up to the podium, I looked out across the crowd of dignitaries, actors and actresses of Hollywood and members of the Player's Guild. I hated the thought that I would ruin this festive occasion but the people of the Earth were out of time and had to know in further detail the dilemma they were about to undertake and face.

As the crowd finally settled down, the attention of thousands of faces quickly turned towards me wondering what was to befall them and would this be their last joyous moment of life on Earth.

It was!

Without hesitation or further adieu, I went right to the point, "Ladies and gentlemen present, today in your presence the battle for Mars and it's Martian moons has ended. The Battle for middle space has ended. The battle for the moon has ended.

The battle for Earth….has begun."

As I continued looking upon the dignified crowd, Tron and Omega entered on stage and stood on both sides of me wearing their silver space gear.

You could hear a pin drop.

The crowd intuitively knew that some of them would be vacating the Earth, some of them would be taken and some of them left behind.

God have mercy on those left behind, I thought to myself.

I told the bewildered crowd, "Today in your presence, you select few will witness for the first time on what has been occurring in space since the Roswell crash. The Roswell craft was an advance guard, a scout craft of Gigantopithecus that we shot down over your skies. You're species, the human species has united with my race, the Anunnaki, which is known in your Holy Bible as the sons of god have joined together to fight against the Gigantopithecus who want to retake the Earth.

What you are about to see shortly in your skies is the remnant of our united space fleet returning from heaven.

Prepare and brace yourselves, thank you," as I walked off the stage.

As the crowd of embellished actresses adorned in their gowns as Greek goddesses accompanied by their dignified actors rose to their feet they looked with curiosity towards the thunderous sounds of an incoming spectacle approaching to their east over the Sierra Madre mountain range. They could see hundreds of black heavy helicopters, Army Sky Cranes with their hospital pods, Marine Ch-53 Sea Stallions, Army Ch-47 Chinooks incoming to the landing field just adjacent to the festival.

The roaring of the heavy helicopters engines reverberated and shook the ground like an earthquake tremor as if the thunder gods themselves were angry…. and they were. The approaching rescue helicopters filled the sky as if locusts from some biblical plague.

As the hundreds and hundreds of military helicopters approached the airfield, an actress yelled out, "Why were all these helicopters marked with hospital crosses on their noses?"

The crowd found their answer within a heartbeat, when suddenly the whole crowd turned in unison to the west in response to thunderous sounds and blinding lights that pierced the cumulonimbus clouds over the Pacific Ocean.

As the crowds looked in wonder as to what they were observing, suddenly in the distance, a handful of flying saucers started piercing the skyline with their laser lights beaming across the sky.

For the first time in their life the people of the Earth realized that extraterrestrial flying saucers do exist and the proof positive was today. As the crowd watched in utter amazement, suddenly hundreds, then thousands of flying saucers permeated the skyline.

The actresses became frightened and grabbed the nearest man for support, while the actors and politicians held on to the dinner table to give them the courage that they didn't have.

As the dignified crowd watched in horror, they then observed what appeared to be thousands upon thousands of flying saucers piercing the sky cover from space.

The women screamed in horror as they watched craft after craft, literally hundreds of thousands of them, trailing smoke, tumbling and falling out of the skies on fire like flaming ambers crashing into the sea.

Many actresses fainted and collapsed when they could see "beings" ejecting from the crafts on fire and falling into the ocean with parachutes that didn't open due to many of the crafts exploding while approaching the landing field.

The male actors and politicians dropped their heads in shock and aghast with despair while others started crying. The remaining guests that could endure didn't say a word as they watched limping and damaged alien craft after craft approach the airfield bellowing smoke and flames.

The air became filled with burning flesh, burnt electrical wiring and kerosene.

As craft after craft exploded in the presence of these dignitaries, their color went from California tan to ash gray in a moment of time as they watched ejecting human body parts thrown into the palm trees and onto the sunbaked sandy beaches.

There was no refuge from the horrible spectacle as human body parts rained down like a meteor shower on these aloft human dignitaries.

The smell of burning flesh and dying screams of humans filled the air as the crowds became traumatized observing this horrible spectacle they were observing.

As the carnage continued the flying saucer crafts were crashing short of the runway. Their explosions threw even more human like body parts through the air splattering the onlooking crowd of celebrities with blood and guts.

In further horror the crowd looked as a blonde female's head landed on the dinner table of a high-ranking politician and ricocheted out onto the airfield tarmac.

As I continued to walk to the airfield to assist, a well-known actor yelled out before the crowd, "My God, Captain Legion, who are these people and where did they come from?"

I grabbed a remote microphone and stated to the remaining few of the crowd who were still standing, "These hundred of thousands of space craft you see in the skies today is what's left of the International Human Space Command of which I am the supreme commander of.

Those "beings" that you witnessed falling into the sea on fire…. are "the son's and daughters of men" who have been fighting and dying from the planet Mars back to Earth!

As I said, the battle for Earth has begun………..and we are losing!

Our enemy, the Gigantopithecus, is much stronger then we are physically and as smart as my race and more warlike then your race.

The human race and perhaps ours is on the precipice of being enslaved by a ruthless and clever enemy who believes without any doubt that they are the true owners of Earth and space.

So now you know the truth, for the Gigantopithecus is coming back to reclaim their planet and enslave you or cast you all out to the cold and barren regions of the Earth where their brothers and sisters, Yeti and the Abominable Snowman have been in hiding for thousands of years.

Remember, the Gigantopithecus believe that God of the Universe had created them for the sole purpose to be shepherds and marshals of this planet. They believe they have been forgiven for their transgressions that they committed before the great flood of Noah and their return and ownership of the Earth is their just redemption.

They, the Gigantopithecus will fight to the bitter death for their right to be here.

That said the human race will have to fight to the death to prevent their enslavement or to prevent themselves from becoming wandering tribal nomads again.

The battle for Earth will be determined in the streets, the alleys, the caves and skies above.

This is one of the reasons why I am here, to start a new species on Mars incase you, the human species lose this war."

Chapter 14-Eden Revisited

In the ensuing days that followed when the Earths crippled battle fleet had returned to fight their last stand, the Gigantopithecus filled the sky with their Death Star ships and began to annihilate the Earths urban cities across the globe, when suddenly, an unknown large human population of the Earth just disappeared and the graves of the dead were opened.

Our advanced sensors picked up that these select humans were being drawn toward the Giant's en masse and in a twinkling of an eye these humans and Giants just disappeared as if they were never there.

The Rapture had occurred!

The remainder of the human population was left in darkness and chaos as the Gigantopithecus continued their attack.

Finally, to avoid total extermination, the Earth's governments that still existed on Earth sued for peace as the first Giganthopithecus Death Star ship landed on the Temple Mount, in Jerusalem.

It was then that the ancient biblical prophecy of old came true as the first Gigantopithecus stepped out on the Temple Mount and told the inhabitants of the Earth that he was their king and if they did not obey him they would be put to death by the ancient art of beheading.

He had a name written across his space suit for it was a human number.... 666...and this was the name of the king who would rule the Earth.

They, the people of the Earth, were then marked on their forehead and branded on their right hand or face death and starvation if they refused. They were also told that a third temple was to be built on the Temple Mount to honor this great king "666" for his great victory over the human hybrids and Anunnaki.

It was in these days as in the beginning, there were *"giants in the earth"* while the *"sons of gods"* wept as they looked down upon the Earth beneath the scorching sun for these fair and beautiful maidens of *"the daughters of men."*

Yet in vain they searched, for they, "*the daughters of men*" were no more for they had returned back to become beasts of burden….again.

In deep sorrow and sadness the Anunnaki left with their select females to the plateaus of Mars to rebuild from the ashes.

As the days passed, I, Frank Legion, would go out on the plateaus of Mars and look towards that silver orb Earth in the light green sky and wonder who will remember what had just transpired in years to come.

For as it is written over time, reality becomes legends and legends become myth for none then will live who will remember it.

So I called forth my pilot, my descendant, my scribe, Rashid Anon, to write down every word I say for posterity so that the people of space and Earth will know what transpired here, for it will be placed in a book called, **<u>The Daughters of Men</u>** and be a *testimonial* to man's beginning and his end.

In the days that followed, as I walked in the cool of the evening in my garden of paradise, I would look into the heavens when Kate walked up to me and looked in the direction of my heavenly stare.

As we looked together at the shining orb while her two little girls played in the Garden of Eden with our newborn son, Adam, Kate asked, "What is that radiant shining object in the western sky?"

I told her, "It is the earth Kate, your home."

As Kate placed her head on my shoulder, she softly stated, "I miss my home Frank."

As I laid my head against hers, I replied, "So do I, Kate, so do I."

Suddenly, Nikki and Oceania walked up to me holding our sons, Seth and Abel, and ask what will happen to the remnants of earthlings who survive this tribulation?

I told them, "The humans will hide in the caves, marshes, desert and frozen tundra. They will live in the wasteland until their redemption draws nigh."

Nikki and Oceania both looked at me embracing our children when I said in closing, "In that day, when we are ready, my people, the Anunnaki and this species that we are creating now will return to Earth and **retake it again!**"

A Proclamation, Declaration and Claim

"I, Rashid Anon, an Anunnaki descendant, and a scribe as directed, as I climb to the summit first and alone, do hereby declare this Proclamation, Declaration and Claim.

We, the Anon's, make Stake, that, "WE", the children of Ankoun, Masgara and those areas near Baalbek, Lebanon are direct descendants of the Anunnaki people from the planet of Nibiru.

This announcement is to make the people of the Earth aware of our presence among you for now 350,000 years.

I, Rashid Anon, further state that as a descendant of the Anunnaki race make further claim that "WE" are the true rulers of this planet and that our heritage *has been stolen* by The Powers That Be, now presently in power.

These ruthless, brutal and self-serving selfish men and women who have obtained power through trickery, deceit, violence and murder have violated our trust by not ruling in good faith as our designated brokers as we decreed long ago.

Therefore, the day of reckoning is now upon the present ruling powers for being a spiritual manifestation and representation for the dark side which is an ancient and evil spiritual power, dominion and principality on high, which rules in darkness and cloaked in secrecy.

You have enslaved our creation, you have failed to read the handwriting on the wall and therefore your time has come and you have been found wanting, *Mene, Mene, Tekel!*

In closing, you will all be removed from power henceforth and cast into utter darkness. For you have been found guilty and condemned to be sentenced to the dark places of the known universe until it's end where you will gnash your teeth in anger.

I, Rashid Anon, do hereby declare that the Earth belongs to: <u>The Anunnaki, The Giganthopithecus, and those select human hybrids that we select to live here</u> and reside with us in peace and harmony with the creatures of the Earth.

This announcement is made to awaken those select humans "with a knowing" from their long slumber and daily confusion of <u>who put them here, why they are here and where they are going</u>.

I, Rashid Anon, a scribe from the Supreme Council in the Great Hall of my people, The Anunnaki, has been ordained and instructed to write this tablet to be placed in the Hall of Knowledge beneath the Sphinx in the Giza Plateau as a testimonial to events that have occurred, are occurring and will come to pass.

In Honored Glory to, The Eternal God, and peace to his people on Earth.

For now it is written and now it is done.

Rashid Anon

***REA

www.ingramcontent.com/pod-product-compliance
Lightning Source LLC
Chambersburg PA
CBHW081209170626
46811CB00010B/3229